Until The Dawn Breaks

S.J. Garrett

CHAPTER ONE

He had never, and would never, understand the compulsion his parents had for driving places when they had the ability to fly. The excuse that they had too much luggage didn't work so well now that he was twenty-five. He knew a cop-out when he heard it.

Gabriel Montreal stifled a sigh and sat back in the leather seat of his mother's beloved Cadillac. "Mom, Dad, I've been resisting the urge, but I'm fairly close to asking 'are we there yet' incessantly. Would someone please at least tell me *where* we're going? Getting thrown into the car the minute I was home from academy was not exactly how I planned to spend my vacation."

Christina Montreal pinched the bridge of her nose and stifled a sigh of her own. She had known this would be difficult, but not only for this reason. "Gabe, please. Try to act like an adult, and a gentleman if at all possible. For ten minutes, please pretend your father and I did not raise a scoundrel."

Her husband, Louis, was driving the car, and he slid a teasing look at her. "And here I thought you liked scoundrels."

"You'll never let me live that down!" she groused. "It was a fling, and he's now very happily married, just like I usually am." She flipped down the visor under the pretext of checking her contacts, but she was looking out behind the car for any potential followers. She had nothing against flying, even though it meant her husband had to use her as an aerial floatation device—no vampyre minded a witch mate holding on during flight—but this was one instance where making a more normal and technically blatant arrival was the better idea.

Gabriel had closed his eyes, but he opened one at the banter. The auburn color perfectly suited his pale blond hair, and it was among one of his best features. "Mom has a sordid past? This ought to be good."

"Shut up, Gabe."

Louis laughed. "Before your mother and I got together, she had a fling with a playboy named Thomas Vincent. The playboy fell rather hard for a lovely witch that Christie met at academy, and rather than get in the way, she almost literally shoved them together."

Gabriel digested that. Then, "Go Mom."

"Gabriel!" Exasperated, Christina turned enough to smack his knee. "Behave yourself!" Her lips couldn't help but curve though. Her son's sassy nature was mostly her fault. "Really, there wasn't much else I could do! Tom and I were certainly not in love, and, *oh,* how he looked at Annie." She giggled. "I don't argue with the outcome! Annie is Louis' childhood friend. I got a great girlfriend out of the deal, and a husband!"

"What tangled webs we weave." He linked his hands behind his head. "I can't say much to any of that, though. Academy can be a tumultuous time. I met a witch at academy in my second year that basically knocked me on my ass emotionally."

"I remember you wrote home about her." Louis glanced briefly in the rearview mirror. "You never said why you broke up."

"It didn't work out." It was all Gabriel offered. He still looked back on those months and wished he had handled things differently. No woman since had ever compared to his black-haired lover. He had tried to find her again, but the academy had been mum about where she lived or even the city where she had been born. "As for my gentlemanly impulses, I will abide by them and be properly dapper and upright while we're visiting your friends."

"Are Ulrich and Griselda arriving soon as well?" Louis asked Christina as he turned the car into the start of a very long driveway.

"Indeed! And they're bringing Liz with them, of course. Lucas will be arriving sometime tomorrow. His parents simply can't get away from their duties, but they've promised to drop everything depending on how things go."

"Why exactly are we here anyway? Just a reunion?" Gabriel asked curiously. "I swear I heard someone mention a wedding or an anniversary or something. I don't complain, but I didn't bring anything *that* formal with me."

Christina studiously studied her nails. Louis cleared his throat. "Something of both, really. It's Annie and Thomas's twenty-fifth wedding anniversary."

"Ah, okay. I was half-asleep after the long trip from academy, so I must have missed the whole conversation." He started to close his eyes, but they opened again quickly as he saw what approached quickly. "Holy hell," he said. "Is that their house? Hang on, let me try again. Is that their *castle*?"

The building sitting in the darkness at the end of the driveway was indeed a castle. It stretched up several stories with at least three towers to be seen. It was probably only less in size than a city block, but not by much. It seemed a stark and imposing sight where it set back into the forest around it, but Gabriel took that with a grain of salt. Most vampyre homes were made to be foreboding so that humans stayed out.

Humans were open-minded and accepting about vampyres, but they still asked the dumbest questions. Gabriel's go-to response was 'read a damn book.' There were plenty of medical treatises on vampyric physiology. He had often envisioned himself getting a castle of his own someday, and the one in front of him got a perfect ten on the charts. He loved it instantly. "I hope they don't mind me exploring the corners. This place is amazing!"

Christina laughed. "I knew you'd like it. And, yes, they won't mind the exploring. Annie says she still hasn't found all the corners herself!" As soon as the car stopped, she hurried out and ran up the walkway to enthusiastically hug the slim woman with red hair that was rushing to meet her in return. "Annie!" she said happily. "It's been years! Oh, I know it wasn't much for immortals, but letters just aren't enough!"

"Christina!" Annie Vincent hugged her with a laugh. "I've been driving Tom mad. I kept pacing at the windows watching for the car!" She shot a smile at Louis as he got out of the car. "Louis! I'm so glad to see you too!"

"But not as much as my wife," he teased her.

"You don't like getting your hair done with me!" She turned to study Gabriel as he got out of the car as well, and a smile tugged at her lips. The young man had his father's striking good looks, but there was a softer sultry appeal that came from his mother. Annie immediately put him on her 'heartbreaker' list. "So you're Gabriel." She smiled. "You favor your father."

"He does." Louis elbowed his son. "Manners."

Gabriel tore his gaze away from the castle. "Sorry." He bowed gracefully with a quick smile. "I'm Gabriel. Gabe for short, if you like. And this isn't lip service: you have an amazing home." He took her offered hand for a quick shake and then bowed again for good measure.

"Very dashing." Annie smiled. "Come inside, everyone!" She lifted a brow as Gabriel turned his head and stared intently at one of the towers. "Gabe?"

"Sorry." He tore his gaze away, a little chill running down his back. "I thought I saw something in the tower. Is this place haunted?" He grabbed two of the suitcases and followed the others inside the castle. "I'd swear I saw something . . ."

"We've never seen any ghosts," Annie told him, "but the curtains have been known to spook people in the right light. We'd get rid of them if we didn't find it funny. Tom and I laughed for hours after a reporter tripped over his own feet to get away." She walked into a brightly lit living room and crossed to where a surprisingly gorgeous man with dark hair leaned against a couch. A lovely black cat lay beside him, and her fur looked a curious glossy color identical to the man's. "Gabriel, meet my husband, Thomas."

After a moment, Gabriel said, "Go Mom, indeed."

"Gabe!" Christina covered her face with a hand. "Thomas, Annie, I apologize. This isn't my son. It's a strange changeling that followed us home one day."

Thomas Vincent just laughed. "Funny, he reminds me of his mother. She's always had an interesting sense of humor as well." He offered a hand to Gabriel. "Welcome to our home, Gabe. It's wonderful to finally meet you."

Gabriel took his hand on a matching smile and decided he could see why there had never been any bad feelings. Thomas was not the sort of person you could dislike. "Thank you." He glanced at the cat curiously and found her watching him with dark blue eyes. She was surprisingly beautiful for a cat, and he itched to pet her. "She's beautiful." He offered his hand so the cat could get his scent.

He wasn't the only one surprised when she hissed very loudly and swiped at his hand with sharp claws. He yanked his hand back in time, but it was only his vampyric reflexes that had saved him. "Yikes!" He took a step back. "I didn't realize she was anti-social."

"She isn't, usually." Annie eyed the cat warningly. "If you're going to act like that, take yourself off."

The cat flicked her tail with the same attitude a woman might toss her hair. With a lithe jump that made her gold collar glimmer, she leapt to the floor and walked out of the room with the regal pride of a queen.

"I apologize, Gabe," Thomas said. "She doesn't usually act like that."

"Don't worry about it. I'm hard to offend." He smiled so that they knew it was true. "May I explore a bit? I won't go peeking into anywhere you don't want me to go."

"The only place off limits is the highest tower," Annie offered. "But if the cat lets you up there, then consider it fair game as well. We trust you, Gabe. You're almost family to us."

"Thanks!"

Christina watched him walk out and then waited a few more moments before clearing her throat and asking, "Does she know?"

"I didn't think she did," Thomas frowned. "We told her we were having guests for our anniversary but we didn't explain everything."

"It's just as well since we both felt so guilty about things!" Annie tossed herself down on the couch. "Such an archaic law we're taking advantage of, and one that should have been extinguished a few hundred years ago!" She raked a hand through her red hair. "Though I guess there are some extenuating circumstances this time that make it better. Still. She's not going to be happy."

"Yes, we got that feeling too," Louis murmured.

Gabriel found himself actually having a good time; the boring trip had taken a turn for the interesting at last. Not only did he think that Annie and Thomas would be fun to spend time with, but they owned one of the most amazing castles Gabriel had ever imagined. There seemed to be hundreds of rooms with dozens of hallways and passages. It even had an indoor courtyard!

Not unusually for a vampyre household, there were no servants. If a room was needed, the owners cleaned it up and got it ready, and they otherwise just hired a cleaning crew once every few months to keep the overall condition nice. The positive to that was that Gabriel didn't have to worry about running into someone and startling them. The negative to it was that he got lost a few times. Three times he found himself circling around and ending up at the base of the largest tower though he really kept trying to head elsewhere. The door was open, he noticed, and the cat sat on the stairs.

He could not shake the feeling that he knew this cat. The eyes watching him were the color of the sky at its deepest point, and they looked familiar. An equally familiar, but haunting, scent from candles drifted down the stairs from the top of the tower. He had never lacked for nerve, so he took a step toward the stairs just to see what happened.

The cat studied him and then turned and walked upstairs calmly. He took that for an invitation and followed her up to the room at the top. Another door stood open, and he stepped inside. He found himself in what looked like a woman's bedroom, and it startled him. It looked lived in and a far cry from the generic, though lovely, guestrooms he had passed before.

A large canopy bed floated off the walls and was piled with fluffy pillows. A vanity sat to one side, covered with makeup and beauty products. A humorous article from the internet had been taped to the mirror, and the headline read *Why You Shouldn't Brush Curly Hair*. All furniture had been made from warm maple wood, and it was the open window's curtains that had spooked him previously.

The cat leapt onto the end of the bed and watched him. He minded his manners, somehow fairly sure the cat didn't like him, though he wasn't sure why. He kept his hands to himself as he looked around, and he didn't poke into anything. The tower had been broken into two large rooms, and the other half was accessed by a door. A peek inside told him it was a bathing room. He very nearly turned away entirely before he spotted a painfully familiar locket hanging from a hook near the door.

His heart clenched as he snatched it up. A flick of his thumb opened it, and the image inside looked familiar and taunting. He cursed violently as he stalked from the room and took the stairs two at a time. Somehow, he made it back to the large drawing room where the others waited, and he demanded, "What the hell is this?" He tossed the locket onto the coffee table between the four older adults, all of whom looked equally surprised at his entrance. "The cat let me in the tower and I found that. What is it doing here?"

Christina picked up the locket and flicked it open. Inside, a picture of her son grinned cheerfully at her with his trademark devil-may-care smile. "Annie, Tom . . . there's a picture of Gabriel inside here."

"What?!" Annie stared at her for a moment. "That doesn't seem possible! Unless . . ." Her eyes narrowed fractionally.

Thomas' eyes had already narrowed, and his expression felt much cooler as he turned toward Gabriel. "Explain."

"Three years ago, while I was at academy," Gabriel kept his voice even with effort, "I gave that locket to the woman I loved. I assumed she had thrown it away when we broke up. How did it get here?"

"Around the neck of a foolish woman," a painfully familiar female voice said behind him. "I wanted to throw it away, but it reminded me that I should not trust my heart."

He turned sharply and found the cat sitting in the doorway. A soft glow enveloped her and then grew taller in height until she was a strikingly beautiful young woman with a cascade of black curls that fell to her waist. Her body curved lushly all over, and her snug dress had splits on each side of the skirt so that tantalizingly shapely legs could be seen. He remembered those legs very well. "Erika." It dawned on him belatedly. "Erika *Vincent.*"

Erika leaned against the doorframe and crossed her arms. "I'm amazed you remembered," she told him. Ice dripped from her musical voice. "You never cared about me the way I thought you did. You might as well have said 'the woman you screwed' rather than 'the woman you loved.'"

He crossed to her and caught her upper arm. Her skin was still soft and warm, fragrant with the scent of her favorite candles. It felt like a miracle to find her again. A second chance. He hadn't thought he would get one. "Let me explain. Please. Just listen to me."

Her palm cracked across his face. "Listen to you?! It's three years too late for that! Take your hand off me, you bastard! I don't want you to ever touch me again!" It only infuriated her more to feel the traitorous shiver of heat rushing through her blood. She hadn't stopped wanting him. She hadn't stopped loving him. He would be her eternal ghost, forever haunting her.

He let her go, if only because his ears were ringing. "Why won't you let me apologize?"

"You cheated on me!" Her blue eyes flashed with magical fury. "An apology will *never* make up for that! You couldn't get back into my bed if you begged! Get out of my house, you louse!"

By that point, Christina's mouth hung open, and Annie's eyes looked as big as saucers. Thomas was, for once, at a complete loss for words, and Louis had the air of a man who really wouldn't have minded a good place to hide. It was Thomas who managed to recover first, but he now knew that things would be far from peaceful. "Erika, my love, you can't throw him out."

"And why not?" she snapped at her father.

"Because you're betrothed to him."

"What?!" The voice was both Erika and Gabriel combined. They stared at Thomas and then turned and stared at each other.

A sudden hot rush of color flooded Erika's face, and she turned on her heel. She stalked down the hall so fast that her hair danced wildly around her hips and shoulders, and she left behind the lingering scent of her skin.

It was a scent Gabriel had never forgotten. It brought back memories of summer days and fall rain. Of countless nights laughing together, of waking at sunset to find her sleeping peacefully in his arms. He could still taste her on his lips when he dreamed. Still breathe that delicate scent of rain and summer. "Damn it." It was little more than a breath.

"Would you like to explain that scene?" Christina asked quietly.

Gabriel turned around and rubbed his chin. It still throbbed, but he knew it was the least of what he deserved. "Erika and I met at academy. I was in my second year, she was in her first. We just . . . meshed. Seamlessly. I gave her the locket for her twenty-first birthday." He closed his eyes. "We were lovers. I . . .." He blew out a hard breath. "I panicked. I realized how deep I was getting, and I was terrified about how much of myself I was losing to her. So I wanted to prove I was still master of my own destiny. I cheated on her."

"Gabriel." Louis just sighed. "You idiot."

"She called me worse when she found out, and rightfully so. Seconds after she walked out, I realized just what an idiot I was. It was too late. She transferred out, and I could never find where she had gone or even where she had come from. Until five minutes ago, I didn't think I'd ever see her again. I also didn't expect her to still be that pissed, though I suppose I should have."

Annie lifted a brow. "And you?"

"I never stopped loving her." He said it simply for it was the simple truth. He sat down in one of the empty chairs and dropped his head into his hands. "What's all this about a betrothal? We're adults."

"You're both still under the laws of the Vampyric Magic Council, and there's an archaic rule that says unmarried members of either gender can be married off by their parents, no matter their age, if their parents feel a pressing enough urgency." Thomas sighed. "And there is an urgency indeed. Gabe, how much do you know about Erika's gifts?"

He started to say he knew she had powerful witchcraft, but it belatedly dawned on him that she had transformed herself, and that was *not* a witch skill. It was reserved solely for vampyres. Yet, when she had slapped him, he had felt the familiar pulse of her magic. That just didn't make sense.

Vampyres and witches had been marrying and producing children together for centuries. A vampyre who mated to a witch and drank his or her blood would become capable of producing children. All children were automatically born witches—human—but they could choose to be converted once they became an adult.

It was a relatively fifty-fifty split for those who made that choice; doing so meant losing all magic gifts in exchange for vampyric ones. Witches who mated with other witches or normal humans would live normal human lifespans, but a witch mated to a vampyre shared their mate's longevity. Annie and Louis were both witches, and Thomas and Christina were vampyres. Gabriel had opted to be converted when he turned eighteen; it hadn't stopped his final maturing, but it had stopped actual aging.

Erika, when he had met her, had seemed to be a witch, though of exceptional gifts. She had both powerful conjuration skills and superficial healing ones, and the twain rarely met. She had expressed no desire to be converted, but now he wondered just why. "How does she have magic in her blood, but she can transform herself?"

"It would seem that she is unusually gifted." Annie sighed. "She was born a half-breed."

"What, literally? As in she's actually half witch and half vampyre and has gifts of both?"

Gabriel stared at her. "How is that possible?"

"We genuinely are not sure. I gather from talking to doctors and geneticists that it *does* happen rarely, but when they said rarely, they sort of said it was the kind of rare that 'only happens on a blue moon that happens to occur the same day as a full eclipse in summer on the fourth Thursday of a month.' That kind of rare."

"It's not too terrible," Christina offered. "Erika is lucky enough to have mostly strengths and few weaknesses. She can transform herself into any feline form, or a bat, can mesmerize minds, and can fly, from her vampyre half. Her witch half has the healing and conjuring magics. On top of it, she can use her voice as another power all together, though damned if we know *how*."

"She could be an absolute danger if she wasn't as beautiful inside as she is out," Louis admitted on a sigh. "She has a sensitive heart. She may hold grudges a long time, but that's only because she can so easily be hurt."

That, Gabriel had known. He felt worse than slime for battering her heart as he had. "So how does all that mean she needs to get married, let alone get married to me?" He rolled his eyes as a thought occurred. "Don't tell me that no one will have her because she's so powerful. Any man in his right mind would leap at a chance to have her for his own. I'm probably the only idiot around here who would trip over his own feet during the leap."

"I'm sure he would . . . except for the part where there's a bloodthirsty cult that wants to sacrifice her on the coming full moon."

Gabriel's forehead hit his palm with a smack. "Yeah, that'd do it." While vampyres and witches normally lived in their own small, nocturnal cities across the world, they still lived in human cities as well, and it always seemed as if at least once a year, some idiot decided to form a cult and try to find a vampyre or witch to sacrifice. It was almost as seasonal as the weather. "Do they need her to be a virgin?"

"That's usually the way it goes," Thomas agreed dryly.

"I will personally attest it is far too late for that, and we both enjoyed the process wholly."

"Good for you," his father countered dryly. "But if you were part of a cult convinced that sacrificing the rare half-breed will make you immortal and give you great power, would *you* believe it?"

"We thought the quickest and easiest thing

would be to get her married," Christina said. "Not even someone dumber than you would think she was still a virgin after marriage, especially if she comes across as fully willing. You were our first choice because our friend Griselda said she saw you in the cards around Erika. Maybe she saw you in her past and we didn't realize. We can't force Erika to marry you if she will be miserable."

Annie watched Gabriel from under her lashes. "There is another option, actually. Griselda's son, Lucas, has been close with Erika from childhood. He's a powerful vampyre himself, and when he heard the situation, he offered to marry her for her own sake."

Gabriel's auburn eyes turned bright green for a moment. "Erika will be mine. I won't hand her over to anyone."

"Then I think you'd better work on getting onto her good side again," Louis told his son politely. "Else it doesn't matter what you will or won't do. The final decision is hers."

Gabriel got instantly to his feet and walked out of the living room to go find Erika. The four parents looked amongst each other and then looked at the locket abandoned on the table. Softly, Thomas murmured, "However, I do think you have an unfair advantage over Luke."

CHAPTER TWO

Erika had opted not to go back to her tower, if only because she knew damned well Gabriel would look for her there first. She instead went to the music room on the other side of the castle. It would take him ages to find her there, if at all. He couldn't even seem to figure out the main area of the castle let alone the other wings.

Yet, she was oddly not too surprised when the door opened some half hour later, and he walked in as if he knew she was there. She didn't look up from the piano she had been playing. "Just like a bloodhound. I never could get far away from you."

The bitterness in her voice warned Gabriel anew that she was far from forgiving him, and even further from being a blushing bride. He walked closer but left several feet between them lest he make her feel crowded. Her nails looked as sharp as her cat form's claws. "You managed to disappear well enough after everything happened," he noted.

"Desperation can do that to a woman. I intended to go back to academy after this year to finish it out. I didn't abandoned my education for you, Gabriel." Her fingers played a poignant chord that seemed to gouge into his heart with anger and frustrated love. "I merely postponed it so I could go back once you were gone and actually concentrate. You ought to be grateful. I never smeared your name or reputation. I let you have the freedom you wanted."

Danger be damned. He had had enough. He moved forward with vampyric speed and hauled her up to her feet with his hands around her shoulders. "You've said your piece!" he bit out. "You will bloody well listen to mine!"

"Is this where you deny cheating on me despite the evidence?"

"In fact, no. I did cheat on you. I freely admit it. What you don't know is *why*." He gave her a little shake when she made a derisive noise. "You were consuming my heart and soul, Erika! I *panicked*. I panicked and I did the stupidest thing possible to find a way to prove I still controlled my destiny. I was in too deep with you, and it scared me."

She stared up at him for a long moment, and then a hint of reluctant acceptance moved in her sky blue eyes. While she may hold grudges for a long while, she was at her core a reasonable woman and accepted genuine remorse—

something she clearly heard in his voice. "Well," she sighed, "I suppose I can't entirely blame you for that. It was scary. Everything between us was scary. Do you think I was any less terrified, Gabriel? I might never have admitted I loved you if . . ."

A bit of humor filled his eyes. "If I hadn't gotten drunk and said I loved you first?"

She winced. "I knew I should have taken that with a grain of salt and kept my mouth shut, but . . . I wanted to hear it. That's why I was so enraged when I found out you cheated. I had taken that risk, thought you had risked with me, and then I found out it meant nothing. Never trust a drunk man," she chided lightly, a little self-mocking. "Lesson learned the hard way."

"So am I forgiven?"

She stared at him for a long moment. "You would have the nerve to ask me that? You think that telling me you cheated on me because you were scared to love me is going to make me forgive you?"

He grinned a bit. "Yes."

The little hint of wickedness to his lips tugged at her in ways she had thought gone. He had always been able to disarm her with his sense of humor. She had more than once, before and after their relationship, likened him to the flame that lured in helpless moths. She had been burned already, and had no desire to be burned anew. Still . . . "Alright. Because I can see reason, and you have obviously hated yourself for your actions more than I could ever hate you, I can forgive you."

"Erika." He lifted one hand to smooth her thick hair out of her face, his fingers lingering warmly and intimately on her cheek. "Thank you."

Her eyes shot up to his, and the promise of her temper stirred anew. "I forgive you, Gabriel," she warned softly, "but I do not accept you as my betrothed. I have no desire for a relationship with you, let alone a marriage to you. I purged you from my system already. Forgiveness you may have. My heart will never be yours again. And neither will my body."

He knew all too well that she was too stubborn to listen to arguments with words. Rather than try, he simply yanked her onto her toes and took her mouth with his. She tasted the same, felt the same. It was as if three years had not passed. He *needed* her in ways he was still only just beginning to understand.

She tried to remain unmoved, knowing his inner decency would make him let her go if she did not respond. She just could not stop the way he made her feel. The scent and taste of him. The feel of that wonderful body pressed against her. She had never forgotten. A low sound of hunger echoed from her voice as she opened her mouth and pressed up to deepen the kiss eagerly.

His hands on her shoulders lifted to fist into her thick curls as he kissed her harder and deeper. Her hands splayed across his chest, and he felt the erotic surge of her magic under her skin. Addicting. Something about her magic had always been addicting to him, and his gut told him now that it might just be the half-vampyre blood inside her.

Only a desperate need for air made them part. Neither could catch a breath, and she was not surprised to see the hint of his fangs through his lips. If you turned a vampyre on hard enough, their fangs came out. It was just as arousing now as it had been in the past. She took a deep breath and pushed herself out of his arms. "Congratulations." Bitterness dripped from her voice. "You proved me wrong. Maybe I didn't purge you from my body." Or her heart, but damned if she would admit it! "I will still not marry you. I do not trust you, Gabriel."

He accepted not only the truth of that

statement, but also the deep pain it caused him. He had destroyed that trust personally. He would have to grow it again. "What about you needing to marry to protect you?"

A bit of a smirk touched her lips. "You're not the only vampyre in my life, handsome. As a matter of fact, I have already received a proposal from Lucas MacDonald. We have been friends from childhood. I will accept that proposal. I know we could be happy together."

Green lit his eyes anew with raw jealousy. "Not the kind of happy you could be with me. We both know we have something special, Erika!"

"And you blew your chance!" she shouted at him. "No second chances, Gabriel! I forgive you for what you did, but I will not trust you! You can stay for my wedding to Lucas should you so wish, but I will *never* marry *you*!"

He grabbed her arm when she whirled as if to stalk away, and bright light flared so hotly that he was briefly blinded. When he could see again, he found himself somewhere near the ceiling, suspended upside down in the air. Magic held him fast, and he could not move. "Damn it, Erika!" he snarled as he saw her now standing near the door.

"Don't piss off a witch, Gabriel. You can either hang there for the next hour, or you can swallow your gargantuan pride and yell for your father or my mother to rescue you!" The door slammed loudly behind her.

Try as he might to free himself, she had bound him in such a way that his flight skills could not get him free. He would be double damned if he yelled for help, but as minutes ticked by he realized that he was getting lightheaded from the position. A hint of sudden humor broke through his temper and humiliation as a realization that Erika had deliberately set him up to take a blow to the pride. If he had been right side up, he could have hung out the hour. Upside down, not so much. There was a saying about getting even instead of getting mad. Erika tended to do both, unfortunately.

Just as he was about to give in and yell, the door opened and Annie walked in. She looked right up at him and visibly worked to conceal a smile. "So there you are, Gabe! Decided to just hang around?"

"Oh, very funny!" he growled. "Get me down!"

"What do we say?" she asked politely.

He seethed and snapped and bit back the feeling of being five again instead of twenty-five. "Pretty please so I can kill your daughter."

She coughed. "I suppose that is close enough." She made a light gesture and broke the rather flimsy spell that Erika had cast. "You're lucky she wasn't mad enough to ensure I couldn't get you free," she scolded as Gabriel flipped around and landed lithely on his feet. "And I came to find you because more guests have arrived. Your rival is here, amongst others."

He scowled. "I don't have a rival!"

"When you meet Luke, you might change your mind, honey. Come along. Erika won't smite you in polite company. Well, unless you open your mouth. You do have your mother's tendency to speak before thinking, don't you?"

Rather than prove it correct, he kept his mouth shut as he followed her back into the hall. Long before they reached the drawing room, he could hear feminine voices lifted in happiness. He recognized Erika's as one of them, and his heart clenched at hearing so much joy inside her. "I just want to make her happy," he murmured. "I want to fix what I broke and prove she can trust me. I would treasure her. Always. I'm not an idiot anymore."

Annie glanced up at him. "And that is why Tom and I are in your corner."

He looked at her in surprise. "You are?"

"I'm sure she and Luke could be happy enough. But . . . happy enough will never be truly enough. I won't lie, Gabe. Learning about your past with Erika in no way changed our minds about why we chose you as a potential husband for our daughter. In a way, it made us feel as if we'd made a *good* choice." She smiled crookedly. "Tom and I and Christina and Louis, we all just thought the two of you seemed as if you would match perfectly. Both hot-tempered, both fiercely loyal, both so full of life. We kind of hoped for love at first sight."

"It happened once." His voice was soft, if only because he felt a bit humbled. "And despite what Erika claims, it hasn't gone away. She knows she will love me the way I will love her: forever. And for immortals—"

"Forever can quite literally mean forever." She nodded. "There's another reason we picked you, Gabriel, though I wonder if I should mention this. It should be Erika's right, but, I just feel you need to know everything." She took a long breath. "It is very, very probable that Erika's half-breed status means she can't have children. She's truly fine with it. She has not yet felt a desire to be a mother herself. I believe Louis said you were similar? That you had not felt a need to be a father?"

He shrugged one shoulder. "I like kids, and I happily spoil my friends' kids, but I don't feel a need for my own."

"Luke wants a houseful." She smiled wryly. "He has enough love for a million kids. He's one of those types."

"Oh. But he's willing to forego that for Erika?" It made him feel some respect for his rival, that he obviously cared enough for Erika to make sacrifices. At the same time, he could also see why Annie and Thomas preferred him over Lucas. With both members of the relationship not wanting to be parents—except by proxy—there would be no underlying guilt. No sense of sacrifice. "Well, I do appreciate the vote of support. I need all I can get! Am I going to have to get tough with Erika?"

She considered her words as they paused outside the drawing room doors. "I think I will sum up by quoting a famous line we all know so well: all is fair in love and war." She grinned. "So if she leaves you literally hanging again, I will not mind rescuing you." She pushed the doors open and walked in saying cheerfully, "I found him hanging around the music room!"

Gabriel pointedly ignored the smirk Erika shot at him and instead focused on the newcomers. Two were a vampyre and witch pair that felt roughly as if they were in his parents' age frame—for immortals, age could only be felt, not seen, since they ceased aging. The female was the witch and the male the vampyre, and the latter shared wavy brown hair and smoky eyes with a younger witch standing near Erika. Gabriel could only assume this family was the one his parents had mentioned also arriving. The final newcomer was the one he felt most interested in, and yet, he found himself a bit surprised by what he saw.

The young man standing beside Erika with a companionable arm around her shoulders was the same five-five height as the half-witch, and he had a relatively slender frame for being a vampyre. His was a deceptive strength, no doubt. He had short blond hair and minty green eyes, and he just seemed to have a permanently cheerful air around him. Gabriel would have absolutely liked him on sight and wanted to be friends, if not for the current situation forcing them to be rivals.

Thomas made a light gesture toward the newcomers and said, "Gabriel Montreal, meet Ulrich and Griselda Percy and their daughter, Elizabeth. Liz is still undecided about converting, so for now, she maintains her witchcraft. The other here is Lucas MacDonald." He coughed.

"And per Erika's insistence when she came in here, Lucas would be Erika's betrothed."

Gabriel gave the Percy family a genuine smile and then turned a tight one on Lucas. "I wish it was nice to meet you."

Lucas didn't flinch back from the bigger vampyre's dark expression. "And I wish you hadn't been such an ass as to create this situation. I suppose we're even."

"Both of you be nice!" Christina scolded. "At least try to keep it civilized!" She sighed. "Liz, Erika, why don't you go get caught up? I'm sure there's a lot you haven't discussed in ages!"

It was a not so subtle hint for Erika to remove herself from the room before there was bloodshed over her. She had no desire to be fought over—and she didn't trust Gabriel not to cause trouble—so she gave Lucas a kiss on the cheek and then linked an arm with Liz. "Very well. Let's go, Liz."

Liz went with her amiably, but when the door shut behind them, she asked politely, "How does it feel to be a prize between two such eligible bachelor vampyres?"

"Don't *even* get me started!" A scowl darkened Erika's face. "I can't believe this situation my parents have gotten me into. And I can't believe the situation that caused them to get me into this other situation!" Under her breath, she muttered, "Everything would have been so much simpler if Gabriel had not come here. Or if he wasn't so determined to pick up where we left off! I refuse to let him hurt me again."

Liz thought for a moment and then offered, "Well, I could play decoy, if you like. I could make a damned good effort at seducing him. At the least, I'd sure be able to distract him. And I wouldn't complain with succeeding. He's rather yummy. Also, succeeding would immediately remove him from your parents' list, so then you wouldn't have anything to worry about! Want me to give a go at it?"

A blend of fury and raw jealousy churned inside Erika against her will. "Not unless you want me to scalp you," she muttered.

Liz started laughing. "Oh, Erika! You're in it good! You don't trust Gabriel, but you don't want to give him to anyone else! Why don't you just give him another chance? Mom saw him in the cards around you, honey, and, frankly, I did too. Your future is as entwined with him as your past."

"Would *you* give him another chance if he had cheated on you just because he was afraid of his feelings?" her friend asked politely.

She thought for a moment. "After making sure he had sufficiently groveled, sure. Then again, I've never learned how to hold a grudge. Except against Marguerite back in grade school. I still entertain fantasies about smiting her if we ever meet again."

"I don't recommend it. I saw her at academy. She converted over and was in the vampyre boxing club. She took a few tournament wins, too."

"So much for that fantasy. I'll go back to lusting after unattainable movie stars."

"Still on that Canadian witch?"

"Have you *seen* her abs? I have such a thing for trained bodies. Please don't let me ever see Marguerite and fall in lust, Erika. I couldn't handle the irony. Bad enough that I spied Luke shirtless that one time and felt uncomfortably as if I was admiring my brother! Tell him to stop lifting weights to save my sanity."

Erika grinned and felt better. There was nothing like Liz's sense of humor to bring her out of any low point she got into. "I'll do my best."

Back inside the drawing room, the air was still a bit tense, to say the least. Griselda shared with her daughter a similar lack of tact and very bluntly told the two young vampyres, "Do us all a favor and go talk and clear the air. I'm not staying in a castle where I never know who is going to try to commit murder in the middle of the night!"

"I'm fairly sure they're not that bad," Thomas told her dryly. "If only because they wouldn't want to hurt Erika. I agree, though." He looked at Lucas and Gabriel. "Get out of here, will you? This entire ordeal is enough trouble."

Lucas shrugged and made a gesture toward the balcony doors. Gabriel went out first, and he found stairs that would lead down into the gardens. He said nothing as he went down them, though he was aware of Lucas following closely. Only when they got out of even vampyric hearing range did he finally ask, "You and Erika grew up together?"

"Effectively," Lucas told him readily enough. "My family lives in Scotland, and the Vincent family has a summer home there. Erika and I met when she was five and I was seven. We just clicked as if we were long lost friends. When I heard about what was happening, I immediately offered to marry her."

"But you're not in love with her?" Gabriel turned to look at him.

"No. I love her a great deal, Gabriel. I would

argue she might be someone I love most in the world. However, that said, I am not *in* love with her. I'm going to do my best to make our marriage work, you can be sure of that, but if we get past the danger, and we decide to divorce, then that'll be fine too. It won't hurt our friendship in any fashion." He continued before Gabriel could speak, "I'm going to be blunt with you, Gabriel, and say something you might find shocking: I am on your side."

Gabriel opened his mouth and then closed it. He could find no words for long moments. "Why?" he finally asked. "I assume you know everything."

"I do. Erika and I don't keep secrets. It was my shoulder she cried on when you broke her heart." He was not at all displeased to see Gabriel flinch at that news. "I don't know your side of the story, but, I do know one thing. I know that you would not still be eligible in Annie and Thomas' eyes unless they felt that you could make Erika happy. To that end, I honestly don't *need* to know your side. I also want Erika to be happy. If she wants to be happy with me, then I will dedicate myself to that. If she wants to be happy with you, then I will be the first to take her shopping for her dress. It's that simple."

Gabriel stared at him. "So you're saying that

you won't interfere with me trying to win Erika's heart anew, or at all be a jealous betrothed? You'll abide by what she wishes, but, at the same time, you'll just quietly say or do nothing to be in my way?"

"That about sums it up. We all make mistakes, Gabe. We hurt others, we make amends, and sometimes we make things better after. Those mistakes make us who we are. Reality isn't easy, and relationships sure as hell aren't. If you and Erika can reconcile, can get through this, you'll come out on the other side stronger than before. To be honest, I don't think that you would have lasted very long even if you hadn't cheated. Neither of you really appreciated what you had until it was gone. Cliché, but too damn true."

"Has anyone ever told you that you have an old soul?" Gabriel asked a bit dryly. He had gone to the garden expecting tension and anger, and he now felt ridiculously calm. Almost zen in some ways. He could very clearly see now what Annie had meant when she had said that Lucas was his rival. Or, more specifically, Lucas could have *been* his rival had he been so inclined. Gabriel felt damned lucky now that Lucas wasn't that at all. "Do you have advice for not provoking Erika's temper?"

Lucas grinned. "Don't do it."

Liz came strolling into the garden with them, and she paused for dramatic effect as both men looked at her with lifted brows. "I am not here," she told them. "I'm also absolutely not telling you that Erika told me to distract you both with my copious charms so that she could head into the village for fresh air. Oh, and I'm also not supposed to mention that she's probably going to the bar to vent her emotions in song."

"She's not allowed to leave grounds unchaperoned," Lucas told Gabriel helpfully. "We know for a fact the cultists are watching the place. Hence why none of us flew in." He watched Gabriel immediately turn and run off at inhuman speeds and then turned to look at Liz. "Is Erika the only one who thinks she should marry me?"

"Actually, I'm pretty sure she's the one who thinks it the least. She's not even on her own side in this one, Luke. Best we can do now is just try to mop up the blood spilled while she and Gabriel probably literally claw their way to harmony."

"And risk getting a claw of our own," he agreed ruefully. "Come on. Charm me as we head back so neither of us feel guilty later."

Chapter Three

The village that sat just beyond the edges of the castle's immediate grounds was technically part of the estate as a whole. It had been under Vincent Family protection for a few centuries. The guard changed every century or so, and not every heir had taken over. Thomas had a great fondness for the village and the people within, so he had taken over for his grandfather. His grandparents now lived happily in another small town somewhere else in Europe. His parents lived in America; they had a fondness for big cities.

Erika had always loved the village of her family's estate. It boasted a population of no more than a few hundred, and everyone knew everyone else. It served as a tourist attraction since it lay between larger cities; people who crossed the country on foot inevitably had to go through the village.

She had been a frequent visitor at the bar since childhood. The owners had always been more than happy to let her steal the stage to sing. The villagers even affectionately called her the Songbird of Vincent Castle. She had never really understood her own gifts, not honestly. Neither witchcraft nor vampyrism could explain the way she almost bent reality just by singing. Flowers bloomed, people with latent skills were awakened into them, and on one really memorable occasion, she had calmed a mob scene just by singing at them. She had been ten at the time.

The flipside to having her musical gift was that it seemed to be fueled solely by her emotions. The more emotional her heart got, the more she felt a driving need to sing and just get it out of her system. The ups-and-downs of the last few hours had her in a fine state. It was barely midnight, and she felt as tired as if it was morning. She wasn't required to sleep during the day like regular vampyres, but she did get damned sleepy. Emotional exhaustion made her feel even worse.

The bar looked busy enough to suit her, and she left the hood on her cloak up since there were plenty of strangers present. She realistically knew that she took a chance because the cultists still lingered around, but at the same time, she knew she was reasonably safe until the full moon. She highly doubted any cultist worth their salt would want to try to keep her for a week when the whole reason they wanted her in the first place was because of her powers.

After a quick talk with the bartender, she

headed over to the small stage along the side. It had an equally small piano at the back. She never knew what would come out when she sat down to play and sing. It was usually entirely improvised, though she had yet to ever stumble over a word or miss a note. Once she started singing, it just came out however it wanted. More unnervingly still, she could then repeat it later on demand, as if she had somehow memorized it immediately.

The first chord she played was no melody of anguish. It was hard, unrelenting, and spoke to the frustration and anger in her heart. She thought for a moment about it being unfair to unleash what she felt on unsuspecting mortals, but then decided that any species who could handle death metal could handle her turbulent emotions.

Regulars in the bar watched her with concern, and the newcomers stared at her warily. Gabriel, who had slipped in unnoticed, felt a bit gut-checked. And when she started to sing, he barely kept his jaw from dropping. He had never actually heard her sing. He knew she loved music, and she had actually been studying it at academy, but he had not realized what her voice could do.

Every emotion she felt seemed to cut through the air and dig into his heart in turn. Only sheer willpower kept him from grabbing her in his arms with a promise to never hurt her again. She might go for his eyes if he tried. He instead stayed in the shadows of the furthest wall and listened to what her song said. It honestly told him nothing new, other than the fact that she was in a more volatile state than he had realized. He couldn't help but wonder if she knew what she unconsciously gave away. The words and music alike held a frustrated anger, yes, but one phrase leapt out glaringly.

Why can't I fall out of love as easily as I fell in it?

She had not purged him from her heart any more than she had purged him from her body. They had imprinted themselves on each other too deeply to ever be free again. He had spent three years remembering the scent of her hair and skin, as if his lungs had been branded by her presence. He knew now that she had spent three years physically remembering him in some way as well. Somehow they had literally left pieces inside each other.

Her song ended to a standing ovation and thunderous applause. She took a little bow and hurried through the bar toward the exit. She felt exposed and unhappy, shaken by what she had seen inside herself. Steps before she reached the door, she felt *him*. Felt the ghostly touch of his hands on her skin and smelled the rich scent of his hair. "Gabriel."

He stepped forward and offered a hand. "You knew better than to go out alone. We're going back to the castle."

She ignored his hand, though she did fall into step beside him to leave the bar. "Liz blabbed," she muttered.

"She did," he admitted guiltlessly. "She worried about you, Erika, and I think we both know she was entitled to that. She told me and Lucas alike, and I volunteered to get you. I would have done that no matter the situation. Think what you will of me, but you know that the last thing I want is to see you in danger."

Her shoulders hunched a bit as she heard a note of pain in his voice. "You're not wrong. Weird as it is, yes, I trust you with my life. It's my heart and soul I don't trust you to have. I have never once thought you would ever want to see me harmed. And I'm sorry if I implied such a thing. You don't deserve that."

He glanced down at her. "Your moods are mercurial, my songbird. I'll never know if you're going to yell at me and leave me hanging in the air or if you're going to be reasonable and give me some leniency. Wish I knew why that was appealing to me."

"Because you're temperamental as well?" she asked with a hint of dryness. She shrugged one shoulder. "I don't feel particularly violent now. Really, I'm just emotionally tired. Tonight has been all sorts of fun." *And you are more dangerous to my heart than ever before.* She felt a little like she had the first time she had met him. She could see the cliff below her feet and didn't know whether jumping would allow her to fly or to fall. Last time, the fall had almost broken her. What would be left of her if she could not fly this time either?

They made it back to the castle and found that everyone else had retired to their rooms for the rest of the night. A key and a map waited in the foyer for Gabriel to get him safely to the room that would be his for the duration of his stay. It was actually not far from Erika's tower, and apparently next to Lucas' room. Not very subtle on the part of Annie and Thomas.

Neither Erika nor Gabriel said anything as they walked through the castle together. They reached his door first, and she told him politely, "Good night, Gabriel."

He paused in the doorway and then nodded. "Good night." The door shut behind him as he went inside.

She immediately turned and went next door. At her soft knock, Lucas opened the door. He looked at her with lifted brows, and she asked softly, "Can I come in?"

"Of course." He stepped back to let her into the room and then shut the door again. "I was just relaxing with a book. Dawn is hours away yet." He took off his glasses and tossed them on the side table beside the chair. "What brings you by?"

"What, no lecture for me going out by myself?" she asked dryly.

"What good would it do?" he asked reasonably. "I can't control you, Erika. It'd be like taming a force of nature. I can make my requests known, can try to impress on you that I really don't want you to do something, but you'll do it anyway if you want, and I can't stop you. Well, I suppose I could be a bit barbaric and toss you over my shoulder, but that might be both awkward and uncomfortable for us both. It's hard to manhandle someone the same height. It's also not my style."

She took off her cloak and draped it over the chair. It had seemed so easy to make her decision, but doubts couldn't help but plague her. "Luke, will you make love to me?"

He studied her in silence for many moments before saying softly, "Erika, you are being unfair to both of us by trying to use me to forget Gabriel."

"Who said that's what I'm doing?" Her hands clenched together. "We're going to be married. We would have a wedding night. We said we would make it work, that we would try to be lovers. Why can't we try now?"

"Alright. I suppose that is fair." He calmly reached out to pull her into his arms. There was a fine trembling inside her body that he knew damned well was not desire. He would try his hardest to make that change, to ensure they both enjoyed things, but he did not hold real hope of it working. You could not force desire where it did not belong, and it did not belong between them, plain and simple.

He slowly leaned in to kiss her, and her eyes closed quickly. The first touch of his lips to hers made her lashes flinch. On a sigh, he framed her face in his hands. "Erika, enough. If you can't even let me kiss you, then we're sure as hell not going to share a bed tonight. You're emotional, you're resisting whatever you found in whatever you sang, and I'm not going to make it worse."

She wrapped her arms around his waist and pressed her face to his shoulder. "I'm sorry, Luke. I should never have come in here. You were right. It wasn't fair to either of us. Next time I come to you, I won't do it with another man on my mind. Maybe you should just surprise me sometime and kiss me without warning. Be all dashing and romantic."

"I'll see what I can come up with." He kissed her forehead. "Off with you. Relax and clear your mind. Things will be much better by tomorrow night." He let her go and smiled as she grabbed her cloak to leave the room. "Good night, honey."

"Good night, Luke." She left the room and tried to resist feeling guilty. It came at her from many directions and was disheartening. She felt guilty for almost using Lucas in a way he didn't deserve, and she felt guiltier still because she just could not shake the feeling that she had been *cheating* on Gabriel. The irony almost amused her.

She glanced at his door as she walked past. The light was on, and a powerful urge rose to find him. Honestly, if Lucas had had half the impact on her as Gabriel, she would have already been married and enjoying her honeymoon. It just did not seem fair that the one she wanted was the one she really didn't want to have.

Her mood had not improved much by the time she reached her bedroom door. Feeling that familiar ghostly touch on her skin as she reached for the knob just stirred up her anger anew. She pushed the door open to walk inside and shot a tight smile toward where Gabriel leaned against her dresser. "Get out of my bedroom. You were not invited in."

"Didn't work, did it?" he countered politely.

"I don't know what you're talking about." She dropped her cloak on the chair. "Get out of my room, Gabriel."

"Did you honestly think that you could make sparks from nothing between you and Lucas?" Mild as his tone was, there was an audible tension that belied his anger and jealousy. And pain. "Did you think it would be suitable revenge on me to sleep with another man right next door to me?" He watched hot red color flood her face and realized the thought had genuinely not crossed her mind. It made him feel only a bit better. "That stung, Erika."

"We're not in a relationship anymore." Her hands curled into fists over her stomach as if to protect from a blow. Why couldn't she get mad? She wanted her temper but could not find it. "I can't cheat on you, Gabriel, if I'm not with you at all."

"Then why do you feel as if you did?" He slowly straightened and began to stalk toward her. "Would it be easier on you if I left? Be easier if I pretended I didn't still love you? Pretended that I don't know you still love me? Tough luck, songbird. Easy won't cut it. It never did. It was never easy from the beginning. It will never *be* easy." His hands closed around her shoulders, and she looked up at him. "Tell me, right now, that you honestly want me to walk out that door and not come back, and I'll do it."

Her lips trembled. "I wondered why I couldn't love Luke, and now I wonder why I can't hate you." She wanted the rage she had felt at seeing him again, the glorious fury from when she had tossed him in the air. She just . . . could not find it. If she had purged anything from her system at all, it had been all of her bitter anger. Her own song had betrayed her. She had been left with nothing but frustration and love, volatile enough on their own let alone when the one she wanted was right before her. "Damn you, Gabriel." She surged up onto her toes and caught his face in her hands as she kissed him with all the churning emotion inside her heart.

Would she have welcomed him if she wasn't emotionally wrought from the day? He didn't know, and he didn't care. She had been given the option to send him away, and she had not taken it. All was fair. He buried his fingers in her hair and kissed her deeper until she made the little sound of delight that always went right to his head. "Last chance," he muttered thickly as he broke from the kiss to nibble at her jaw.

She knew full well the potential consequences of her actions. Even if she could not yet trust him with her heart, she knew she could trust him with her body. That had never been a problem for them at all. She wanted to give him the words he needed to hear so that he knew he was truly welcome, but the only words she felt on her tongue were three words she could not say again. Instead, she got to work unbuttoning his shirt.

He made a sound something like a tortured groan and kissed her again and again until her fingers grabbed desperately for the edges of his shirt to support her when her legs went weak. Need. She had never felt such a ferocious need inside herself, or inside him. She wanted to tell herself it was the abstinence, that it was just the passage of time, but she knew it was a lie. They had both changed, and that had changed everything between them. For the better? There was no knowing yet.

He tore from the kiss and then groaned when her mouth closed hotly over his neck. "You going to bite me?" he asked roughly. "I assume you need blood, being half-vampyre." His breath hissed out when her sharp incisors teasingly scraped his skin. His entire body felt painfully hard and aching for her heat and softness. "I'm not going to be responsible for my actions if you bite me, songbird."

"Promise?" She laughed a bit breathlessly as he fiercely stripped her dress up over her head. Her underwear and bra hit the ground only seconds later. "You still set land speed records for getting me naked." She yanked his shirt down his arms and watched hotly as he shrugged out of it. Liz would have had a hot flash if she had seen Gabriel shirtless. Powerful muscle moved sensually under pale skin and tempted her fingers into touching. She slowly spread her hands across his strong stomach and then slid them up his chest. She had never realized how tactile she could be until she had met him.

His auburn eyes burned as he returned the favor and softly cupped her breasts. The nipples tightened in response, and she caught a breath. His fingers squeezed gently just to tease and then slid down her torso. She couldn't stop a moan when his rough fingertips scraped over the sensitive skin along her ribs. As much as she liked when he touched her breasts, it had always been her ribs that lit her nerves up when he caressed her.

He kissed her again greedily while his hands continued to torment her tender flesh. Her nails bit briefly into his chest and then dropped to fumble with his belt and the button of his slacks. She got no help from her lover; he was too busy making her feel as if she was about to self-combust. She finally got everything undone and shoved the pants down his hips. He was naked underneath, as she had expected, and a husky laugh caught in her throat.

His lips left hers so that his sharpened incisors could nip at her neck. "What's so funny?" he asked thickly.

"I appreciate convenience, that's all." Her delicate fingers skimmed along his throbbing erection and made his breath hiss in. "All mine."

"Always yours." His fingers fisted in her hair and dragged her head back. "There's been no one else these last years, Erika."

Perhaps it was the rough way he said it. Maybe it was the look in his eyes, the hunger as wholly emotional as physical. Whatever it was, it planted the first seed of new trust inside her heart. She believed him. Maybe there could be a chance for them after all. "As long as there is no one else in future years," she countered unsteadily. "That's all I want."

"You're all I need." His hands curved around her hips and then lifted her off her feet entirely. She coiled her legs around his waist and held on as he swung around and strode toward the bed. He lowered her to the soft mattress and felt his heart quiver as her hands nearly would not let go of him. "I'm not leaving you. I can't." He sank into her arms and kissed her desperately. "Hold onto me."

She could only clutch at his shoulders as he slid down her body with more of those wonderful hot kisses. His fangs scraped down her ribs, and she cried out with pleasure. Her legs parted to make room for him, and her entire body arched wildly at the first wicked caress of his mouth on her most tender flesh. He remembered all too well how to drive her mad. Her breaths became sobs and her nails dug into his shoulders. "Gabe!"

He slowly made his way back up her body,

dropping stinging kisses as he went. Her leg hooked over his hip and then she gave a quick surge of strength and rolled him over. As she pinned him, his entire body quivered with desperate desire. She never looked more beautiful than when she was like this, rumpled and flushed and so perfectly his. He tried to reach for her but she slipped through his grasp to slowly caress her way down his body. His teeth clenched together as her lips and fingers trailed a blend of heat and erotic magic.

She tormented him the way he had tormented her, mercilessly and yet with a need only to give pleasure. She knew just how much he could take. Knew the way to kiss him so that his eyes darkened, the way to scrape her nails so that he gave that wonderful groan. His hands grabbed her arms just when she expected, and her breathless laugh spilled out as he dragged her up and rolled over to pin her again. She had never imagined déjà vu could be so deliciously wonderful.

Her legs coiled around his hips as he positioned himself and then thrust deeply into her body. That first lunge ripped a moan from her that echoed his. They still fit together. He drove into her again, and then again, savoring how she felt around him. She moved beneath him with equal power, taking him as deeply as he had taken her.

Her head tipped back and bared her throat unconsciously. He badly wanted to sink his fangs into her lightly tanned skin. He had never done that before. It was the ultimate intimacy between vampyric lovers, and he had fought it. He knew, now, that she had surely fought the same. She hadn't even told him she was half-vampyre, let alone implied she *could* bite him until now. "Let me have everything," he pleaded thickly as he shifted position so he could take her deeper. "Give me freely everything."

She coiled her arms around his shoulders and arched up to bare her neck on purpose this time. She could manage only a needy whimper as his mouth closed over her pulse. The slicing sting of his fangs sinking in was only pleasure, and she heard herself sob his name. Ecstasy boiled up wildly, powerfully, and ripped through her body in waves of sheer delight she had not remembered. She clung onto him with all of her strength, and his entire body shuddered in mutual pleasure as he buried himself one last time and let the release consume him, too. He dropped onto his elbows and then settled his weight fully against her as they both slowly relaxed.

It was only when she felt him nuzzle her neck that she bothered to stir, and even then, it was only to tilt her head for easier access. His tongue swept across the bite mark, and she felt a little tingle through her skin that told her the bite had closed. She had always thought it nice of nature to ensure a vampyre could heal their bite, and now she decided it was even nicer of nature to make it feel pretty damn good. She let out a long sigh of contentment. "Don't ask me to move," she murmured huskily. "I'll stay here all day."

"Does that mean I'm invited to sleep here?" he countered just as huskily. He found the strength to lift himself up, and his eyes devoured her sleepy and satiated expression. "No kicking me onto the floor and making me go back to my cold and lonely bed?"

"Not this time." She stretched languidly and then looped her arms around his neck. "You can stay as long as you like."

He knew it was a test, and he felt a bit humbled that she would give him chances to prove himself worthy of her trust. Waking at the next sunset together would shift things from being potentially just a one-night-stand to the start of a more serious relationship. "I have no intentions of going anywhere." He slowly disentangled their bodies and shifted to lay beside her. She turned onto her side toward him, and he draped an arm over her waist. Dawn was only an hour or two away; he felt it in his bones. "No wonder," he murmured.

"Hmm?" She didn't open her eyes from where she had snuggled closer.

"No wonder you had the same internal clock to tell you when sunrise and sunset came. I just assumed you were subconsciously planning to be converted and therefore picked it up early. I think . . . that perhaps you didn't trust me enough back then, either."

She opened her eyes at that and looked up at him with a smile more wry than bitter. "That day I found out you cheated? I had intended to tell you that night about me. I had it all planned out how I would tell you everything and ask you to come meet my parents. And then I saw you with that other girl, and . . ."

He winced. "I screwed up harder than I thought I did." He searched her eyes. "We can make this work, Erika."

"Well, we'll see." She closed her eyes again. "At the least," she added sleepily, "we've always been good together here."

He waited until she had actually fallen asleep

before leaning down to tenderly brush her lips with his. "We've been good together everywhere," he murmured. "And I think we're both finally ready to accept that." He tugged the blankets up over them and closed his eyes on a long sigh. He was already asleep when the sunrise came, but not even the deepest sleep of a vampyre could make his grip on his lover loosen.

He would never let go again.

Chapter Four

Erika woke just a bit before sunset and felt a warmth all through her body. It slowly spread through her heart and soul as well, as she felt Gabriel's body curled around hers and his arm over her waist. It didn't feel as if he had let go even once. Heated memories from years before came back to her, and she braced herself for the pain from them.

There was none.

She said nothing as she stared at the closed curtains and the hints of the sinking sun coming in around the thick black material. Had she really let go of all the pain and bitterness? In twenty-four hours, she had gone from feeling violent and enraged to feeling calm and accepting. Her own temperamental nature often did that to her, though. Gabriel had called her mercurial because he couldn't predict her moods. She could so rarely predict them herself. For all she knew, they would be in another fight before dawn and she would either yell at him or magically smite him—or both.

Darkness had begun to replace the reds and golds. Gabriel stirred, and his lips feathered over her shoulder. He snuggled her closer against his chest and murmured thickly, "Missed you. Missed waking with you. You haunted me."

She could have brushed the words off with a flippant retort, but he deserved better than that. She had made the decision to try to trust him. He was still there, he had not let go, and in his sleepy state, he was giving her a look into his heart that she had not had before. Honesty. If they found nothing else, they needed at least that much, especially if she intended to marry him for any length of time.

"I often called you my eternal ghost," she murmured. "I could still feel your hands on me. Still smell your hair and skin. Maybe that's why I was so . . . furious when I saw you yesterday. I had almost convinced myself that I was free of you, but your presence reminded me anew that I never would be. Then you kissed me and it reminded me of more things I wanted to forget. I honestly don't know if I was mad at you when I smited you, or if maybe I was mad at myself. I kissed you back, Gabe."

He propped himself up on an elbow to study her relaxed face and tangled hair. He skimmed a finger down her cheek. "And you then promptly told me you were going to marry someone else, and you very probably would have if you hadn't hung yourself with your own rope. You owe Lucas an apology, songbird."

The pet name was entirely new to her; he had never really used a personal endearment with her before. It had been another layer of intimacy that had instinctively scared them both, as much as his biting her had been. That he willingly embraced both now helped continue healing her wounds and made her trust slowly blossom more. "I know." She sighed. "Though I'm pretty sure he won't at all complain with this outcome. He was probably on your side all along."

He kept his mouth shut on that one. "Were even *you* on your side?" he asked politely.

After a moment, she started laughing. "In hindsight, maybe not." She reached up and smoothed her fingers over his beloved face. "I think if I had a more calm personality, we would have sat down very reasonably yesterday, talked, and potentially decided to try again. I meant what I said about forgiving you. You did something damned stupid, to be sure, but you did it for a reason I can understand. I don't know if I might not have thought of the same thing if . . ."

"If you didn't so intensely dislike being touched by people other than family anyway?" He shook his head affectionately. "The first time I decided to kiss you, I likened it to attempting to pet a porcupine. You've only got one way to do it right, and if you get it wrong, you're going to regret it in painful ways. You have no idea how damn relieved I was when you kissed me back."

She should have been offended, but she found the analogy too hilariously appropriate. She had never been a touchy-feely-physical type person, and in fact intensely hated when strangers or even just mild acquaintances touched her even in passing. She liked and enjoyed hugging and being cuddled by her parents or grandparents, and Liz and Lucas, but that had been the limit of it. With Gabriel, though, all bets had been off. "The moment I saw you, I had the immediate thought that the sooner I had your hands on me, the better. I was rather happy to think I might be able to have and enjoy a physical relationship after all, and so when you decided to seduce me, I only feigned reluctance."

"I figured that out when I kissed you. It took barely a second before you were wrapped around me like a clinging vine. Did we actually make it to the bed?"

"No, but you said the carpet was surprisingly comfortable." Memories that would have before hurt her now just brought humor. "And we were both a bit flummoxed by the fact that our first kiss turned into the first time we made love. I think maybe that's when we both started getting a little scared."

He leaned down and kissed her tenderly until she sighed into his lips and melted into his arms like candle wax. "And rather than discuss it rationally, we just kept on going and pretending we weren't scared, while all the time we were just losing ourselves more deeply into each other until love wasn't an option and was instead *mandatory*." He sighed. "Luke was right. We could never have appreciated our relationship back then. We were just too immature and not ready for things."

A delicate black brow began to slowly lift. "Luke said that, did he?" Her tone stayed mild. "You mean you two discussed our relationship, and he literally aligned himself on your side?"

He laced their fingers and tangled their legs together. Not that that would stop her magic if she lost her temper. "Maybe."

"Oh, don't look at me like that!" she snorted. "This porcupine got thoroughly petted just perfectly last night and feels too damn good to bother with anger over something she can't resent." She felt a laugh welling as he bent his head and pressed a deliberately sultry kiss to her neck. "You don't have time for that! You need to get back to your room to freshen up and get new clothes before we have breakfast."

"How much time do I have?"

"An hour total? Therein."

"I can borrow ten minutes of that."

Her eyes widened. "Ten minutes?" she echoed. "What can you accomplish in ten minutes?"

The answer, she decided as she staggered into her shower eleven minutes later, was *a lot*. She thought that it should be physically impossible to get turned on that hard and fast, but boy was he good at utilizing time! Her body still throbbed with the aftereffects, and she suspected she might look more than a bit loved. A glance in a mirror confirmed it. She definitely looked as if she had just gotten out of her lover's bed. Maybe a shower would tone that down. The last thing she wanted was to walk into the dining room and have her mother ask if she got laid.

She made it down to the dining room first, and she could hear her father's merry whistling from the large kitchen. Christina was in there with him, chatting over something or another, and Erika could also hear Ulrich and Griselda offering a hand. In the Vincent castle, there was no such thing as too many cooks spoiling the broth. The making of meals was as much a family deal as the eating of them, even though technically only a few members of the family actually ate food. She had always jokingly likened it to a diabetic baker. Just because they couldn't eat what they made didn't mean they didn't enjoy the process.

"Good morning, Erika!" Christina said merrily as she walked into the dining room with the coffee tray. She suddenly stopped in her tracks, stared intently at the younger woman, and then coughed. "Er, coffee?" She put the tray down and beat a hasty retreat back for the kitchen. In a low voice that Erika still heard, she whispered, "Tom! Your daughter slept with my son!"

Not bothering to temper his tone, Thomas countered, "Good for her. Ask her if she wants bacon."

Erika dropped her head onto the table as her shoulders shook with laughter. And people wondered where she got her personality from! "Yes!" she called. "Some bacon would be nice. I need protein!"

"I can't imagine why," she heard Ulrich murmur drolly.

Annie and Louis came into the dining room

from another direction, their arms full of flowers for the table, and both stopped to look at Erika. The latter lifted his brows. The former asked politely, "How are we this morning, sweetheart?"

Erika was beginning to be fascinated. She had been utterly sure that no one would see any of Gabriel's lingering effects on her. She had taken care with the shower and her makeup alike, and she had looked utterly normal as far as she could tell. What kept giving her away? It wasn't as if she had some sort of psychic billboard, was it? "Hungry."

"Imagine that." Annie handed off the flowers to her daughter. "Please put these in vases." She then grabbed Louis' arm and hustled into the kitchen. "Thomas!" she whispered. "Have you seen your child?"

Liz walked in the dining room door as Erika was putting the flowers where they belonged, and the fortuneteller paused for a long moment before asking her friend, "Okay. Which boy got lucky? Luke or Gabe?"

She got her answer when the two men in question walked into the room from the other door, and Gabriel's gaze went right to Erika with an intimacy that could be felt. His eyes heated clearly as they slid down her body, and a hint of pink climbed her face that was assuredly not embarrassment or temper. Whatever might have been said was put on hold, however, as the elder generation came in from the kitchen with trays of food for the witches in residence and fresh glasses of blood for the vampyres.

"Good night?" Griselda asked Erika warmly.

Exasperated with everyone, Erika planted her hands on her hips and swept a look around the room. "I know damned well what I look like, so I want to know what the hell is giving me away! I'm not smiling stupidly, humming, or doing any of those other ridiculous clichés! What in the name of the gods has all of you so damn sure I got laid?"

"You're wearing yellow," Thomas informed her politely. He handed her a plate. "You never wear yellow unless you're feeling happy, and considering the state we last saw you in last night, I can't imagine you'd be happy for any reason other than Gabriel being in your bed. No offense to Lucas."

"None taken." Lucas accepted a glass of blood and eyed the toast wistfully. The only thing he missed from pre-conversion was carbs. He loved breads. "If I had the ability to make her that sort of happy, we'd have been married years ago."

Erika just sighed. "Okay, fine, yes, Gabriel was

in my bed. And, yes, I'll take him as my betrothed instead of Luke. We're going to try again." She looked at Gabriel, and though she smiled easily enough, those who knew her best could see that there were still hurdles to be overcome. "We did a lot of talking. Cleared things we could have cleared yesterday if I hadn't been so mad at myself."

"Not at him?" Christina asked as she sat down next to Annie. "I think he deserved your temper."

"Thanks, Mom," Gabriel groused and took the seat beside Erika. "You're not wrong, but I think we were *both* just as mad at ourselves as at each other. It's very probable that our future will be periods of bliss pocketed with moments of yelling, fighting, and flying spells."

"Was that how it was before?" Liz asked. She scooped up a heavy heaping of biscuits and gravy.

Erika snorted. "So to speak. I don't remember actually casting anything on him before, but that might be because I didn't want to do damage to my dorm room, or his." She bit into a piece of bacon with a ferocious crunch. "All bets are off now. But, you know, I think I'm okay with the fact that we can piss each other off that much."

Lucas smiled at her. "That's because you both

enjoy being mad. You like being temperamental. There's really nothing wrong with that, not when you don't hurt anyone that way. You would never lose your temper with Liz the way you do with Gabriel because you know she loathes conflict and you wouldn't want to hurt her. And, well, you can't lose your temper with me because I refuse to let you have that satisfaction."

"Does he even *have* a temper?" Gabriel asked Erika.

She grinned up at him. "We call him Vampyre Buddha, if that says something." His hand smoothed over her leg under the table, and she hesitated before letting her hand cover his and lace their fingers together. "Maybe I should just go into town and be obvious about things. The cultists might see me, realize I got laid, and give up their plans to sacrifice me." She pursed her lips. "I wonder what happens if they set up a ritual and fail to have whatever they need. I mean, would it backfire at them? Imagine if they needed a blonde and grabbed someone who dyed their hair. I wonder if they'd get karmic backwash from a bad spell."

"As if they wouldn't get karmic backwash from sacrificing a living being!" Griselda snorted. "And if we're all lucky, you won't get anywhere near them to find out the truth."

Thomas nodded with a smile. "We intended to send out the engagement and wedding announcement to the paper tonight. Annie's parents and mine are on their way and will get here the day before the wedding."

Which was only six days away, on the full moon. Erika felt a bit daunted to realize that in a week she would go from single, to reconciled with her ex-lover, to married. Was a week enough to learn to trust him, or would they spend their honeymoon working on that? Would there *be* a honeymoon? She frowned at Gabriel. "Where are we going?"

It dawned on her that she should clarify her statement, but he seemed to just know what she had actually asked. "I wouldn't mind somewhere they have long nights so we can enjoy more time together," he mused. "Maybe Alaska. It's beautiful there. You like the snow." He saw everyone staring at him, Erika included, and he blinked. "What?"

"You understood her?" Annie asked.

"Obviously. What's your point?"

She looked at Erika. "She has this terrible tendency to think to herself and then pop out with a statement or question and expect us to know what she's referencing. She's learned to backstep and fill in details, thankfully. You're the first person I've seen who can understand her thoughts. You're not telepathic, are you?"

"No." He tugged affectionately on Erika's curls. "I think it's just that we have a terrifyingly similar way of thinking."

"Terrifying is one word for it," Louis agreed dryly.

The rest of the night went surprisingly peaceful. Wedding plans kicked into high gear now that the groom had been confirmed. Annie and Louis sat Erika down and made her make decisions about what she wanted for her wedding. Never the type to suffer alone, she dragged Gabriel into the conversation. It was as much his wedding as hers. It would be no small affair, either. Members of both families would come out for it, and the entire village had been invited, too.

By the time they dispersed for the rest of the night to get some peace before dawn, Erika's head swam with colors, fabrics, flowers, and cake options. The latter had been made her choice alone since Gabriel obviously couldn't eat any.

"I'll just enjoy watching you enjoy it," he teased her as they walked through the castle.

Without pausing, he continued, "Am I staying in my room, or am I invited into yours?"

"I think it would be utterly ridiculous to pretend we need separate rooms, and to pretend you wouldn't climb the tower and sneak into my bed anyway even if I said you couldn't stay with me," she retorted. "Do you want to live here after we marry, or does your family have a home you prefer?"

"I'm in love with Vincent Castle. I wouldn't mind living here." He cocked his head. "Who will inherit it?"

She smiled. "Mom and Dad have talked about having another child sometime soon. So, presumably, if I get a sibling, the lineage would carry through him or her. You and I will take care of it for as long as we like, and then it'll pass on if we find someplace better for a forever home. Maybe we'll end up loving Alaska."

He just felt happy that she was thinking in terms of forever. As he put his clothes back into his suitcase to move to her room, he evaluated his words and then said, "I won't give you a divorce, Erika. Not without a fight. I'm stating it now. I'll write it into the wedding vows. I'm making this commitment for *good*, and not just until we confirm you're off a cultist hit list."

"I want to believe you."

"It won't be that hard to prove." He shut the suitcase. "Trust takes enough time to build without needing to rebuild the foundation first." Seemingly changing the subject, he added, "I need more clothes. I'll have to have my things shipped here. They aren't really going to make me wear that ridiculously floofy shirt as part of my wedding ensemble are they?"

She coughed and led the way up to her—their—tower. "Vampyres like tradition. We haven't updated our wedding style in a century or two. At least you're not in a corset."

"Why do you need one? I love your body, and I thought you did too."

"Sure, but like pantyhose, corsets are sometimes required to wear certain things I couldn't wear otherwise. Also, you know, accuracy. Just think of the fun you'll have getting me out of it on our wedding night." She stripped off the betraying yellow sundress and tossed it into the hamper. Hot hands curled around her waist and tugged her back against a hard chest. "Gabe?" She tilted her head back against his shoulder, sensing something serious inside him.

He turned her around so she was forced to meet his eyes. "Erika, let me in. Let me prove myself to you. Give me a second chance. Give *us* a second chance. You've been flippant about it so far, saying we're trying again, letting me in your bed. There's still a huge wall between us. I can see it, let alone feel it. I need the words." His hands slid up to frame her face, and his auburn eyes churned with emotion. "Please. Tell me you'll give us a true second chance, that you'll try to believe it when I say I love you and want to be with you."

She drew an unsteady breath. Flying or falling. She didn't know, but she knew she could no longer stand on the cliff wondering. Nothing he said or did would make any difference if she didn't at least step forward and *try*. "A second chance." Her powerful voice quivered against her will, belying her uncertainties. "I'll try, Gabe. I'll try not to automatically look for hidden meanings in what you say. And I'll accept it when you say you love me. I won't try to use our past just to hurt you when we're angry." She couldn't keep looking at the hope and joy in his beautiful eyes. It was unfair. "If I ever tell you I love you, it will be said when I can say it knowing that I trust you to keep my heart safe."

He hauled her up onto her toes and kissed her with a famished heat that once more turned her muscles to wax. The embrace lingered, and lingered, until she finally had to break free to gasp for air. Only his arms held her upright. "What you can do with ten minutes," she managed to say weakly, "should be illegal."

The local paper waited on the doorstep the following night, and the front cover article had a photo of Erika and Gabriel with the big announcement of their coming nuptials. As Liz studied it at the breakfast table, she asked, "Did it occur to anyone that this might throw oil on the fire and have the cult maybe become aggressive?"

"The last time someone tried to put a siege on this castle," Thomas said mildly without looking up from his beloved comics, "was when America was still colonized. And not even a few thousand could breach our walls. I'm fairly sure a handful of lunatics won't be any more successful."

"So the songbird is in a cage until she is married?" Christina asked dryly.

"Tweet tweet," Erika muttered under her breath. "I don't know why I can't go out if I just bring others along. Gabe can turn into any canine form and start biting people, and Luke can mesmerize others."

"So you have Canis?" Ulrich asked Gabriel curiously.

"And flight," he confirmed. "I admit, before I found out that the cat I met here the first night was Erika, I thought maybe the Canis part was the problem. Some cats just don't like me, the same way some vampyres with Felis are not liked by dogs." He shot a grin at his fiancée. "Maybe that explains us. We actually *do* fight like cats and dogs!"

Everyone at the table had to laugh, even Erika, and she swatted at him with her napkin. That sense of humor inside him had always been one of the things that drew her the strongest. He could be charming, debonair, and the perfect gentleman, but there was always a rakish edge to him. She could honestly say he had never swept her off her feet, yet there was no denying that she had fallen hard and fast. Physical desire aside, they wouldn't have ended up in bed so damn fast if there hadn't been more behind it.

"So what are the plans for tonight?" Annie asked. "Louis and I are going to make phone calls to some shops in the next big city and start ordering deliveries for the wedding. Tom, you're going to call the cleaning crew in for the other guestrooms?"

"I am. They can come in tomorrow while we're all sleeping. They're wonderfully tidy and quiet alike. Suppose that's what happens when the company is run by a witch. After that, Tina and I thought we'd commandeer Ulrich's building skills to start figuring out how to set up the gardens for the ceremony."

"Luke and I are in charge of calling the caterer and band." Liz propped her chin on her hands. "And while we all say we get vexed by old traditions, can I say that I don't mind this one where the betrothed couple just has to make decisions and enjoy themselves? I look forward to that myself eventually. It's stressful enough without having to do all the work! How do humans manage this?"

"Sheer luck in some instances," Lucas told her wryly. "But that rule applies for *betrothals* and not normal engagements. The idea being that the couple is being forced to marry, so why force them to do work? You will very probably find yourself in a normal engagement, Elizabeth, so you may have to do work of your own."

"And she will enjoy every minute," Griselda murmured. "She likes being bossy."

"Takes after her mother," Ulrich murmured back. "What about you, Erika? What are you and Gabriel up to today?"

"He wants to explore the castle and see if he

can figure out the key to not getting lost." Erika smiled. "Me, I think I'll play around with some music." She felt no guilt at all about saying it; it wasn't a lie, after all. She just didn't have any desire for them to know what she and Gabriel were really going to do, especially since she'd had to play dirty in order to get Gabriel to agree to what she wanted.

Everyone dispersed after breakfast to get started on their plans, and Erika and Gabriel initially headed as if to go to the next floor. They instead diverted partway and used one of the many back halls to leave the castle entirely. Both grabbed cloaks along the way but did not wear the hoods.

"This is asinine," Gabriel muttered as he took her hand with his and escorted her toward the small road that would go into the village. "And don't think you'll be able to use your body to always have your way."

"I'll be able to use it to have my way when you don't really find anything objectionable about what I want," she retorted, "and we both know that it goes the other way as well. You are very aware of the fact that I completely lose all control when you touch me."

He grinned a bit wickedly. "You're welcome."

She snorted softly and then grew more serious. "Thank you. For this. I need to sing, Gabe. When they said a music agent was here on vacation and had offered to judge a competition for fun, I knew I had to enter. I just want a chance at maybe a record. It's ridiculous, I know, and I know I'm immortal and have plenty of time, but there are so few immortals in mass media . . ." She sighed. "It's a silly dream."

He brought her fingers up to his lips. "Hey, look who you're talking to, Erika. I'm the guy with a degree in fine arts. We're lucky enough to be born into wealthy families where we can do whatever we like, but we both want to make it on our own. If your voice is on a radio, or my paintings are in a gallery, it'll be because we worked for it, not because we asked our parents to call in a favor. So, yeah, I was willing to be seduced into accompanying you to this contest. What will you sing? Something original, or a cover?"

"Don't expect a love song dedicated to you."

"Perish the thought! I'm more inclined to expect something like *Miss Independent* out of you."

She thought about it. "That would definitely fit me, to some extent. I actually rather wanted to fall in love. I just didn't find someone that I could fall for. That's different from deliberately keeping a distance. I was actually thinking about *Before He Cheats.*"

He winced with wry humor since he knew well she was just teasing him. In fact, he found it a good sign that she would make jokes—real ones, not false ones—about their past rather than try to pretend it did not exist. She had said she would not use it to hurt him, and now she went the extra step to make it less important than their future. "That's one of those songs where you shouldn't condone the singer's actions, but, damn, do you think she's justified. And if you're singing it? I'll watch the room and see who starts looking scared. We'll know to warn their significant other that they might have a cheater of their own."

The bar was packed to overflowing. People had come in from nearby bigger cities just for the contest, and the windows had been opened all the way so that people could cluster outside and watch or listen. Gabriel found a spot inside where he could watch—he ended up behind the bar— and Erika went to get into the queue for performing.

The total number of contestants had

remained small, thankfully. All of them were surprisingly talented, and Gabriel overheard the bartender telling a patron that the owner had tried to cut down on the number of gag performers by asking for a small sample as an entry fee. It meant that everyone in attendance was more likely to enjoy themselves, especially the agent who had willingly volunteered for the judging. She had made no promises about picking up the winner, but she had made it clear that she was always looking for new talent.

A hush fell on the room when Erika finally took the stage. Even the first chord from the band providing backup was enough to send a chill through the room. Despite the teasing between her and Gabriel, Erika had picked her music deliberately to not just draw on her emotions and make her stronger, but to also showcase her natural skills. She belted out a Celine Dion song that could have been written for her—and Gabriel.

She took her bows amid the cheering and applause and then made her way toward the bar where Gabriel waited. He leaned across the top, caught her face in his hands, and kissed her quite thoroughly, sending up a new wave of cheers and laughter. "Well done, songbird," he murmured huskily. "Do you need to stay for the rest?"

She shook her head. "No. The award will be announced tomorrow during the day. If I win, I'll find out tomorrow night. Let's get out of here." A shiver ran down her body. "I don't feel safe for some reason."

Proof of her half-witch blood. Most witches had a finely tuned sense of danger, which had kept them and their vampyre allies alive for a millennia. Gabriel had never doubted a witch who sensed danger, and in light of the circumstances, he sure as hell wasn't doubting his lover right then. He leapt over the counter and kept her tucked under his arm as they made their way quickly toward the closest exit.

They made it halfway home before Erika stopped in her tracks and her pupils widened to consume her blue irises. Gabriel immediately wrapped his cloak around her with the intent of flying them back to the castle, but he was too late. Several figures in hooded cloaks and masks emerged from the thick trees and moved to surround them. All were armed with spears or swords, and Gabriel barely stifled a sigh of disgust.

"Yeah," Erika muttered against his shoulder, "they're not the brightest torches in the basement. Not a single arrow among them, and would you believe they dislike guns?"

"Then why are we worried?" he muttered back.

A huge blast of necrotic energy landed near their feet and blew out the stone and dirt violently. Gabriel cursed darkly as he held Erika closer protectively. "That's why," she told him under her breath. "Remember the 'bloodthirsty' part of their description? They've sacrificed several of our kind to access some nasty magics."

"Hand her over, vampyre," one of the members warned. A robotic cadence to the voice meant identity was impossible to determine, and implied the use of a mechanical disguiser. "Give her to us and you can go free."

"You are joking, right?" Gabriel asked politely. "You honestly think that I'm going to just walk away and leave anyone, let alone my fiancée, with you lot?" Red moved across his auburn eyes warningly. "I recommend getting lost." He dropped his voice. "Buy me a minute to transform. I bet I can clear them fast."

Erika swiftly evaluated her options and then decided that the simplest answer was usually the best. She took a step away from Gabriel and deliberately made it look shaky as if she was afraid. She took a long calming breath and then poured all of her power into her voice as she began to sing. The fury of her song made the ground shake, and cultists yelped as they lost their balance.

Light swept over Gabriel, and the cultists did not realize what he had done until they heard the first snarl and saw the large pitbull lunging for them. Some people reflexively screamed. Another tried to lob a blast of energy that missed entirely. Most started running. Gabriel went after those who tried to stand their ground, and he narrowly missed getting one in the ankle.

As the dust settled, and Erika stopped singing, she looked around at the scene and was almost amused. A dog. Of all things to scare them away, it had taken a large dog. These people who murdered shamelessly for power had screamed like children and run from a *dog*. A big dog, though, and a rather powerful one with a formidable reputation to start with, so maybe she could understand their fear. Attempting for humor, she patted her leg and called, "Here, boy!"

Gabriel turned from sniffing at a weapon that had been dropped and shot Erika a heated glare. He stalked toward her and turned back into a man as he approached. "I knew this entire idea was asinine!" he snarled at her. "What if they'd had guns? Vampyric speed can't outrun projectiles at the speed of sound!"

"Well, excuse me!" she snarled back. "I didn't realize that they'd be stupid enough to attack me if I wasn't alone! *You* agreed with me!"

"*You* had your hands on something sensitive at the time, and I wasn't thinking!" He moved with shocking speed and grabbed her around the waist. Before she could do more than curse, he had her across his shoulder and was flying back toward the castle. "I don't care if you have a contingent of knights in armor, you are not leaving the castle again until after we marry!"

"Put me down!" she shouted. She saw the direction they headed, and her temper flared more. "If you think you're going to be in my bed after you've manhandled me, think again, Gabriel Montreal!"

Down in the gardens, Thomas and Ulrich watched the couple fly by overhead. After a moment, Ulrich told Thomas, "You're right. I can't think of a more perfect match, either. Pity they won't have kids."

"No," Thomas disagreed dryly, "we're *lucky*. The world only needs one Erika and Gabriel."

Gabriel flew right in the large, open windows of the balcony and walked over to drop Erika on the bed. She instantly bounced up and came at him with a pillow. He let her get in several good licks before he disarmed her and tossed the weapon aside. She took a breath to rail at him more, but the words were lost when he caught her face in his hands and kissed her with an aggression she had never felt before.

Temper turned into a firestorm of hunger. She dragged in a ragged breath when he finally released her, and the breath came out again on a moan as his fangs sank into her pounding pulse. "Is this how we'll end every argument?" she managed to ask. "Because I could handle that, really."

By the time dawn made its approach, they were snuggled under the blankets together. Heads at the bottom and feet on the pillows, though, because they were using the blankets like a bed-bound fort and watching a movie on her smartphone. Just because vampyres and witches kept old traditions didn't mean they didn't love modern technology. They just used it more sparingly, and hid it more convincingly.

"The mirror in the grand family room hides a flat screen," Erika told Gabriel as she cuddled closer against his side. "Friday nights are movie nights." She sighed contentedly and rested her chin on her hands. "I think I don't mind that our future will be pockets of bliss mixed with yelling and fighting. Because the yelling and fighting ends with amazing make-up sex, and the bliss involves blanket forts and re-watching *Avengers*."

He laughed. "No spells this time."

"Maybe next time. And . . . I'm sorry. The idea was dumb."

"And I'm sorry for going overboard."

She grinned. "Was that us being reasonable?"

"I think it was." He sighed and draped an arm over her back. He couldn't seem to stop touching her. "I did mean what I said. I understood why you wanted to go, and I was willing to be seduced into agreeing. I think we both should have just taken things more seriously."

Very solemnly, she said, "I promise to stay in the castle until after we're married and not even an absolute moron would believe I'm still a virgin when I've got a vampyre this damned gorgeous for a husband."

"I'm still vexed at how they find that to be of any value anyway."

"Right? And they call *us* old-fashioned."

Chapter Five

Three days left to the wedding, the entire castle seemed a bit on edge. No one honestly knew whether or not the cultists would be stupid enough to launch an attack, and the sort of bad magic they packed implied that it might be a bad idea for *anyone* to go outside the castle at all.

People were beginning to arrive for the wedding anyway, so things stayed busy. The guestrooms had been scrubbed clean and quickly gained occupants. It also wasn't unusual for old acquaintances to show up just with well-wishes even if they did not intend to stay for the nuptials, so when Annie told Gabriel he had a visitor, it was not a surprise. He had already seen at least five other old friends from academy and earlier, and that had been just that night! Erika had been kept busy with people she knew, too.

When he opened the doors, however, his entire body tensed slightly. "Terry."

The redheaded vampyre on the front step shot him a beaming smile. "It's been years!" she agreed. "I heard you were getting married and just had to come find out for sure! Is it true you're marrying a half-breed?"

"I'm marrying Erika Vincent," he countered, bodily blocking the doorway so she could not muscle inside, "and she is half-witch, half-vampyre, yes. I assume we have your good wishes, Terry?"

Brown eyes narrowed sharply. "You aren't going to invite me in, Gabe? How utterly impolite of you for someone you used to be close with."

Manners told him to step back and let her in. Self-preservation told him to tell her to get lost. Manners, unfortunately, won. He stepped back to allow her inside. "Do not cause a scene," he warned in a low voice. "If only out of respect for the Vincent Family. They are one of our oldest and most honored."

"I would not cause a scene," she retorted stiffly. "I merely wish to attend the wedding as a guest."

He believed not a single word of it. Still, he shrugged one shoulder. It was not yet his castle, and Annie and Thomas had said all were welcome as long as they had rooms left. Considering guestrooms numbered in the hundreds, it would take a while. "Fine. I'll show you to a room." He spotted Lucas approaching and had never been so grateful to see anyone. "Luke! Meet Terry Gordon. She and I went to academy together for my first year there."

Lucas had never been accused of being dumb or slow. He evaluated the entire scene in just a second and then casually stepped over so he walked between Gabriel and Terry. "It's a delight to meet you, Terry. I'm Lucas MacDonald, Gabriel's wedding attendant and an old friend of his bride. Will you be staying with us?"

"Of course." Friendly though her tone sounded, her eyes shot a dirty look at Gabriel that he had not made Lucas leave. "Where are you staying in this wonderful place, Gabe?"

Casually, he said, "One of the guestrooms on the left side near a tower. They gave me the room next to Lucas." He stopped in front of another guestroom and opened the door. "Here you are, Terry. You can unpack your suitcase or just live out of it. The dressers are kept empty for whatever preference of the guests. I suppose we'll see you at lunch."

She glared at him for a moment before becoming all smiles again. "Of course. I can't wait to meet this Erika!" She went into the room and shut the door.

Lucas looked at the door and then up at Gabriel. "This ought to be interesting." He caught Gabriel's elbow to pull him away. "I notice you lied about the sleeping arrangements. I assume you don't want her to go poking around the tower."

"I notice you assume she would," he muttered. "I'm sure you guessed, but, she and I were lovers before I met Erika."

"Please tell me you didn't dump her *for* Erika."

"No, I dumped her because she was getting clingy to the point of almost feeling like a stalker, and it creeped the hell out of me. She's a few years older, thankfully. She graduated the same year Erika started, so they never crossed paths." He scowled. "Terry has made a point of contacting me over the last few years, making it very clear she wants to get back together. No amount of politely telling her to leave me alone did any good, and neither did threatening to have a magical restraining order from the VMC cast."

Lucas winced. It said a lot about things that Gabriel had considered going all the way to the Council for a spell that would ensure the subject literally could not get within a few hundred yards of him. "So it would be entirely logical to assume she is not at all here to wish an ex-lover a happy wedding and is instead likely intending to either cause trouble or at the least try to 'steal you back'?" He smiled suddenly. "You ought to tell

Erika. I'm sure she would be happy to handle things. Loudly. And possibly violently."

"Don't tempt me! That's the only reason I won't tell her; Thomas made us promise no bloodshed before the wedding."

"Is that why you've gone at least a day without fighting?"

"Mom bet Annie that we can't make it forty-eight hours without an argument. We both want her to lose."

Lunch began starting at eleven pm, and all vampyres and witches in residence came to the immense formal dining room for it. Annie had gotten smart and hired some local cooks to come and stay through the wedding to help feed all the witches. Additional blood supplies had been ordered from the Council's closest contact. Lucky for vampyres everywhere, donations were as common for them as for medical emergencies.

Erika knew there was a potential problem the moment she spotted Terry. She immediately grabbed Lucas' arm and hauled him to the side. "Why is she here?" she asked bluntly. "And before you ask the obvious, yes, I know who she is."

He lifted a brow. "May I ask how you know?"

"I was warned about her from the moment I started seeing Gabe those years ago. She never showed up, but I made sure I had info about her so I knew who I was watching out for. Is she here to ruin our wedding?"

"That seems to be the consensus," he agreed. "Gabriel said he didn't think he had the right to throw her out because it's not his castle yet."

She nodded briskly. "Warn Christina she's very probably going to win her bet. This could easily get ugly. In the meantime, I have a point to make." She firmly walked across the room to Gabriel and snuggled against his side intimately. He automatically put an arm around her without stopping his conversation, and she internally smirked as she saw Terry glaring at her.

As far as she was concerned, she and Gabriel would have a quick conversation so she could reassure him he absolutely had authority to eject people, and they would get rid of the problem before it became one. "Meet me in the garden after lunch," she whispered in Gabriel's ear. She nipped at his lobe teasingly and then sauntered away.

The witch Gabriel had been talking to bit his lip to hide a laugh as Gabriel stared after Erika with visible longing. "Everyone said it was a betrothal, but you two look pretty happy, all things considered. It's a love match after all?"

Gabriel chose his words carefully. "Our parents wanted us to meet because they thought we'd hit it off, and we did. Love at first sight, so to speak."

Immediately after lunch, he headed out to the gardens to find Erika. His ability to always find her, what she now jokingly called his bloodhound nose, served him well enough to tell him he had gotten there first. He leaned against a hedge wall and contemplated the merits of eloping. Not that he didn't think the wedding would be a great memory, he just thought everything would be made easier if he and Erika eloped and *then* had a ceremony. It wasn't likely to happen. All of their parents had insisted on tradition.

"Hello, Gabe."

His body tensed anew as he spotted Terry walking toward him. "I'm waiting for my fiancée," he told her curtly. "Whom I happen to love with all of my heart. I'm not sure how much plainer I can make things for you. We're done. We've *been* done. I'm very happily getting married in three nights."

"You don't love her." Her lip curled into a sneer. "You cheated on her before, if I recall."

"I believe everyone is entitled to a mistake or

two. That was my second. The first was ever dating you. But, then again, maybe dating you is what allowed me to realize Erika was special." Certainly, he had seen the significant differences between the two women and the way he felt for them, and that had no doubt leant itself to his fears. "There's nothing to rekindle, and I'm pretty sure that if I asked my future father-in-law, he would be happy to use his influence on the VMC to ensure I get that magical restraining order against you."

Fury lit her eyes. She heard a footstep and shot forward with vampyric speed. Before he could evade, she grabbed his face in her hands and planted a hard kiss on his mouth. He grabbed her shoulders and shoved her away, and disgust lined his face. It changed almost instantly to horror, and she looked back to see Erika standing a few feet away. The half-breed's face was expressionless.

Terry immediately smirked. "You just can't hold onto him, can you? You may as well call off the wedding now, Erika. You know he'll get bored of you again."

Blue eyes seemed to stare into her soul briefly and then stared into Gabriel. Without a word, Erika swung around on one foot and walked away calmly.

Gabriel felt more than a little alarmed for more than one reason. That was *not* his Erika. Where had her temper been? She hadn't looked hurt either, which implied she knew the scene to be a false one, but she had walked away rather than fight. What if she was too hurt to show it at all? He shoved Terry aside and snarled at her, "If you hurt her in any fashion, I will break you apart!" He ran after Erika but found himself unexpectedly waylaid by Liz. "I have to find Erika," he told her.

In a surprisingly loud voice, she countered, "No, you're going to your room to remove yourself from the scene. Get some rest, relax, and worry about Erika later. Trust me, Gabe." She dropped her voice much softer and added, "Seriously, trust me."

He hesitated and then nodded a bit. Somehow he didn't feel at all surprised when she immediately took him toward the tower rather than his old room. He *was* surprised to have her shove him onto the stairs and then shut the door firmly. "Hey!"

"Calm down," Lucas told him dryly from where he sat on the steps. His friend turned, and he smiled. "Don't worry. Erika knows what she's doing, and she's decided that she's going to make sure Terry doesn't ever entertain the idea of bothering you again."

"She didn't believe that scene?" Gabriel had never felt so relieved in his life.

"Definitely not."

Erika not only didn't believe the scene, she was also disgusted by it. She found it horridly distasteful for anyone to force themselves on someone unwilling, and Gabriel had looked miserable and angry when she had walked up on the lip lock. If any part of her still wounded heart tried to tell her she might have been imagining his expression, she told it to shut up. She was going to trust Gabriel, and she was going to trust her instincts *about* Gabriel. He had opened up to her over the last few days in ways he never had before. His willingness to have a whole relationship, to put no walls between them, had just made her trust grow.

She knew there was something inside her, some lingering unease that kept her from full trust and finally telling him she still loved him. She just didn't know what it was or how to fix it. Was it something he needed to say or do, or was it all on her? Maybe it was leftover fear from the past. If things had been intense and profound before, they were doubly so now. She had known from the first night that things had changed between them, and each passing day made it more obvious. If she was falling, not flying, and he did not catch her, there wouldn't even be anything left of her after she landed.

Her feet made no noise as she headed for Gabriel's old room. She listened outside the door and then smirked a bit as she opened the door and strode in. "You are too stupidly easy to predict."

Terry yelped and clutched her robe closed. Half-undressed, and now embarrassed, she could not find her bravado. "Oh, am I in the wrong room?" she tried to bluster. "It's such a big castle. Let me just put my clothes on and you can show me the right one."

"On the contrary, I'm here to show you the door, and I care not if you're dressed or naked." She snapped up a hand and shot magic across the room. "I'm going to make it painfully clear." The spell had hoisted a horrified Terry into the air, and Erika now magically towed her out into the hall. She didn't bother to keep her voice down, either. "Gabriel is mine. He made that choice, and I trust him. You are a sad and pathetic individual who thinks she can have any and everything she wants."

Doors had started to open, and people came from all corners. Terry turned red in humiliation. "Let me go!" she pleaded.

"Sorry, but we don't keep vermin in the house. You crossed a line, vampyre-breath." Erika mercilessly marched her down the hall and toward the main entrance, well-aware of the amused crowd following. "You showed up uninvited just to cause trouble. You tried to force your attentions on a man who doesn't want you. You were just now lying in wait in the room you thought was his, intending on a seduction either willing or forced."

They had reached the door, and Erika released the spell from several feet up. Terry shrieked as she landed on the stairs on her ass and then slid down several more painfully. She clutched her robe closed as tears ran down her face at seeing all the gathered people watching the scene. She almost thought it couldn't be worse, but then Gabriel walked up behind Erika and tugged her back into his arms. "Gabriel!" she begged. "Are you going to let her treat me like this?"

"You earned it." He tossed out her suitcase so that it landed with a thud beside her. His voice was calm if only because his anger had entirely been replaced by sheer humor. He had a feeling he would never forget the sight of Erika dragging Terry down the halls magically. He would have *paid* to see it again. In fact, he had seen cell phones. Maybe someone had recorded it. "Thanks for stopping by. It wasn't a pleasure. Stay very far away and don't make us get that magical restraining order. I hear they can be pretty painful if you breach them."

She grabbed up her suitcase and stumbled as she ran down the stairs at high speed. Erika watched her go and then looked up at Gabriel. "Does that qualify as taking out the trash, or being relatively cat-like and protecting my territory?" She looked into the castle as she heard applause and saw the crowd. She scowled. "Get lost! Show's over!"

"Best wedding I've been to yet," one older vampyre quipped cheerfully as he ushered his family down the hall.

"One wonders if we'll make it *to* the wedding at his point," Gabriel muttered under his breath. He kept Erika close and turned her toward the hall that would lead to their tower. "We need to talk."

"About what?" she asked him curiously. He said nothing, and she kept quiet until they were in the peace of the tower. "Gabe, what is there to discuss?" Reasonably, she reminded him, "Your relationship with her was before me, so it has no bearing in my mind, and everything that happened tonight was entirely not your fault." She thought about it. "Except for not throwing her out immediately. As far as I'm concerned, this is enough your home that you can do that. So maybe you're a tiny bit at fault. A few percent."

"When she kissed me and I saw you, I just had this horrible vision of losing you again," he admitted in a low voice. "Especially when you didn't lose your temper the way I'm used to you doing. I thought maybe you had been hurt too badly for temper."

"Gabriel." She tenderly framed his face in her hands. "I said I would give you a second chance and try to trust you. I am doing that. Trust means not assuming things. It means thinking before acting. I said I would believe in you loving me. Did I feel an initial pain at seeing her kiss you? Of course I did. But I forced myself to be calm and look twice." She grinned suddenly. "And, really, logic alone told me it wasn't how it seemed. Your face gave it away. You looked less like a man kissed by a woman he wanted than a man who had just been forced to drink lemon vinegar."

"That is a disgusting sounding concoction." He paused. "And not inaccurate." He pulled her into his arms and pressed his forehead against hers. "Thank you," he whispered. "For still trusting me." He wanted to ask what more he could do to help her feel safe and secure, but he just felt that if she knew, she would have said something. That last hurdle, whatever it was, was invisible, and it could trip either of them at any moment. "Do you want to have dinner with everyone?"

"No." She kissed him lingeringly. "We can ask for a tray. I want to stay here with you until dawn. The chatter will die by tomorrow night so things can be normal again." She caught a breath on a laugh as he scooped her up into his arms. "How very dashing of you, sir. Much better than being over your shoulder."

"You found it thrilling." He dropped her onto the bed and then leaned down to cage her against the covers.

"Absolutely not." Absolutely she had.

"Liar." He kissed her hotly until she melted in his grip.

"Okay," she whispered huskily against his lips, "maybe I am."

T-minus two nights to the wedding meant

the decorating started. Things were, indeed, as normal as they could be in a castle with fifty guests, but people still laughed and talked about the scene with Terry. The betrothed couple took it with good humor, and Gabriel bribed someone for a copy of the video she had made. Erika just laughed at him for wanting evidence.

It actually did not become obvious that there was another problem entirely until Louis and Christina noticed their son didn't drink anything for breakfast, and he reached the sluggish side by lunch. The symptoms of unintentional starvation looked fairly clear. Christina grabbed Thomas to go talk to Gabriel, and they found him watching gardeners starting on the décor for the ceremony.

"Gabriel." Christina caught her son's arm and turned him around. "Are you okay?"

He frowned at her. "Why wouldn't I be?"

"You haven't eaten anything all day," Thomas pointed out. "You got a glass at breakfast with the rest of us, but you didn't touch it beyond a first sip. I assumed initially that you must have bitten Erika and weren't hungry, yet it's approaching lunch, and you're definitely showing the effects of not eating. What's going on?"

Until the question had been asked, Gabriel had honestly not noticed a problem. He rubbed the back of his neck. "Now that you mention it, I think the problem was the taste of the blood. I didn't like it for some reason."

Christina and Thomas exchanged a look. Carefully, the former asked, "Gabe, you *are* drinking Erika's blood on occasion, aren't you? I'd assume you must be. It's very rare for a vampyre to *not* bite the one they love."

"We never did in the past," Gabriel said slowly, "because it was an intimacy we feared. This time, from the first night, we accepted that. So, yes, I've been drinking her blood almost every time we make love. Not a lot, though, so it shouldn't hurt her."

"That isn't at all the concern." Thomas shook his head. "I think you've lost taste for any blood but hers. I had wondered if that might not happen, particularly since she is so very special. That blend of half and half inside her is *potent*. You told Liz the other night that Erika's magic was oddly addicting, and you suspected the half-vampyre blood inside her—especially her mesmerize gift—was at fault. Is it that far of a stretch to think that drinking her blood could be just as addicting? Your appetite for regular blood has fallen off dramatically, and since you're not getting enough from Erika, you accidentally starved yourself."

"It's not a bad thing," Christina offered reasonably. "Erika, being half and half, has the benefit of eating real food and therefore takes in all the nutrients needed to make her blood a viable source of nutrition for vampyres. And she very obviously does not mind at all that you've been biting her. I'm sure we'd have heard if it were otherwise."

Gabriel hesitated a bit. "We're still rebuilding our trust. And that . . . that's an entirely new level. It makes me completely dependent on her. It might make her feel better about things, but it might also make things worse." He paused and then asked softly, "She needs blood, too, doesn't she? At least some. Where does she get it?"

Thomas and Christina exchanged a smile. "Ask her," Thomas said softly. "You might be surprised by how well things seem to be falling together perfectly for you two. In the meanwhile, you had better either go ask her to feed you, or plug your nose and choke down some normal stuff before you pass out. I'm fairly sure you don't want to see your fiancée's bedside manner for someone who got sick for a foolish reason."

"Good point." He watched the other two vampyres walk away and then immediately made his way through the gardens toward where he knew he could find Erika. Perhaps her blood might also explain his 'bloodhound' sense for her. He had always had it, even in the past, but it had gotten ridiculously more powerful lately. It wasn't just the pieces they had left inside each other; it was her blood inside him. He couldn't help but wonder what might happen if she bit him in return. His gut told him that her resistance to doing so might be another sign of her still flagging trust.

He had just spotted Erika cutting roses for decorations when the garden wall was struck by something powerful. The entire stone structure shuddered, and the grounds shook equally. Gabriel was moving before he was conscious of it, and he grabbed Erika in his arms to rush her away from the wall. "What the hell!"

"A cultist," she told him curtly. "They sensed me. I guess they didn't realize the castle is fortified for just such a thing. It's not like they can climb over a twenty-foot high wall. I'm thinking whoever lobbed that found themselves unpleasantly getting shocked in return." She sighed deeply. "I will be very glad when this is over!"

"You and me both." He started to let her go, but dizziness swamped him and he staggered.

"Gabe!" She caught him hastily, though his weight threw her off balance and they ended up on the ground anyway. "What's wrong with you?" she demanded. Her heart pounded wildly as he slumped against her breast. "You feel so weak! You skipped breakfast, didn't you? I was wondering about that. Why the hell did you do that, you idiot?"

He had no strength to lift his head. "Not intentionally. Promise." His voice was quiet, his words a bit slurred. "Erika, I can't stand the taste of any blood but yours anymore. And I don't drink enough from you to compensate for missing meals. At least . . . s'what Mom and Thomas think."

She could only sigh. "Is that all? Honestly, Gabe. You should have immediately said something to me."

"Intended to. Cultist attacked, though."

"Then, in that case, I forgive you." She tenderly smoothed his hair from his face. "I don't mind, Gabriel. I really don't. I'm enough witch that I can help you, since I eat normal food. I can be your meal ticket."

The affectionate term made his lips curve. Witches who willingly offered themselves as a food source to vampyres had adopted the moniker. He had always found it cute. He gathered his strength and lifted himself enough to reach her neck. She aided by bending closer over him, and it almost seemed as if there was something protective in her posture. Her sigh sounded long and contented as his fangs sank into her skin. The act of biting was always intimate, whether it was passionate when it came while making love, or simply beautiful and emotional when it came in this way.

As his strength returned, he eased up more without releasing her, and his arms went around her. She slid her fingers through his pale hair contentedly. "I like this," she murmured huskily. "You needing me." His fangs left her skin as his tongue tenderly closed the bite mark with the wonderful tingle of magic. Leftover magic, she decided, from when he had once been a witch. Such a curious thing. "Get enough?" she asked. "I don't notice a difference."

"I feel better than I have all day. In a while actually." He sat up entirely and tugged her onto his lap. Logic said they could be found by anyone, and it was inevitable someone come looking because of the attack, but he didn't care. He brushed curls out of her blue eyes and smiled. "Can I ask something?"

"Of course."

"Where do you get blood? I know you have to. You never answered me before about that."

She bit her lip. "Because it's a bit odd, and I worried what you might think." She sighed. "I can only drink vampyre blood. Weird, right? It's supposed to be that vampyres have to drink non-vampyre blood, because non-vampyres eat food and their blood gets the nutrients vampyres can't get personally. But, for some reason, maybe because I *do* eat food, I need some strange component of vampyre blood. Maybe it keeps me from getting sick. We don't know, not really. And . . . you won't like where I get it."

"Luke?" he guessed. He smiled when she looked up at him quickly. "I would have guessed Liz if she had converted. She hasn't, so it had to be Luke. I'm not jealous, Erika. Strangely, I haven't been jealous of him except for that first night when you tried to put him between us, and even then, it lasted only until he and I talked." He thought for a moment. "Would I work?" he asked seriously. "Could you use my blood, even if I'm using yours?"

She frowned slowly as she thought about it. "That . . . actually seems logical. You get nutrients from me that I get from food, change it into whatever it is a vampyre needs, and then I get that from you." Her gaze lowered as thoughts churned. She had fought the urge to bite him because it had been a level of trust she could not find. The last intimacy. Yet, that fear felt fainter now that he had placed so very much trust in her hands. If she denied him blood, he would *die*. That was a hell of a thing.

He deserved the same, and she wanted so badly to remove all barriers between them. Sometimes trust took conscious actions, she thought. Maybe this was the final wall between them. Could she say she loved him after it? Would she finally feel safe knowing she was flying and not falling?"

He caught a breath as she leaned up and nipped at his pulse. "Be gentle," he told her in a husky, teasing voice. "It's my first time."

"Ooh, a virgin. I begin to see the appeal." She sank her fangs into his skin contentedly and let herself enjoy not just the wonderful taste of his blood, but the utter feeling of *rightness* that swept through her soul. Words trembled on her lips as she closed the bite and eased back, yet they would not come out. "Gabe."

He tugged her up for a kiss that seemed to make a million promises. She fell into it willingly before realizing she could see, sense, *something* hovering inside her mind. A door. She could see a door. She did not know where it led, and so she kept it shut. *Why can't I tell him I love him?* The words cried out inside her mind.

As if he had read her thoughts, he released her from the kiss and caught her face in his hands. "It'll come," he promised huskily. "I can wait. You're with me, Erika. That's more than I ever dreamed I might have. Are you happy with me?"

"Yes," she vowed instantly. "Don't ever think I'm not."

"Then it's enough for now." He kissed her again and then got to his feet and tugged her up. "Let's finish getting the roses we need. Lunch isn't too long away, and you'll need food." He bent and nipped at her neck. "I'll take my lunch in bed later."

"Down boy," she laughed. "Come on. Let's go." Her eyes wandered to the wall that had recently rejected an attack from death magic. "Desperate people do desperate things."

"And are dangerous," he agreed. "We'll get the roses and then tell everyone what happened."

CHAPTER SIX

The night before the wedding, grandparents and other family members finally arrived. The castle had become something of a madhouse. Rising tensions and stress levels meant that bride and groom alike were sniping at people, and their attendants felt honor-bound to prevent violence. If it looked like Erika or Gabriel were getting overwhelmed, Lucas or Liz would grab them and hide them for an hour or two until things calmed down.

"It works," Liz told Annie dryly after stashing Erika in a quiet and unused guestroom. "I think we should be *really* glad that she and Gabe aren't actually in charge of things. You would be kept busy patching everyone back together."

"How bad is she?" Thomas asked curiously.

"She was in cat form when I found her, she hissed at me for grabbing her, and her tail was probably breaking the speed barrier after I tossed her in the room and shut the door. By the way, she clawed me. Can I have a heal?"

Erika was still an unhappy cat when the guestroom door eased open half an hour later. Her blue eyes stared at the opening with an unblinking stare. A hand came around the edge, and it held a veil. "Don't bite!" an amused female voice told her. "I bring pretty things for you to get fitted in!"

Her mood immediately improved. Erika leapt to the floor and then glowed as she became a woman once more. "It's safe, Grandmother," she said dryly.

The door opened entirely, and the lovely vampyre came in with suitably dramatic flair. She looked no older than her son or granddaughter, and could have almost passed for Erika's sister since they possessed similar black hair and blue eyes. Vincent genes did pass along strongly, after all. "There's my girl!" Maria Vincent said happily as she hurried forward to hug Erika. "You look wonderful, my darling." She eased back and caught Erika's face in her hands. "You're happy."

"I am! Enough so that I'm *this* close to thanking the cultists. How weird is that?" She sighed with happiness as she accepted the veil being offered. "I can't believe you're letting me wear this."

"It's been worn by every bride of the Vincent family for a few centuries, whether she is of blood or marrying in. It will look utterly spectacular on you. I also brought along my old corset that I was married in, and that your mother borrowed as well." She winked saucily. "I'm sure Gabriel will love it as much as my Jon does. Speaking of," she continued blithely, "he said he was going to impart words of wisdom to Gabriel about dealing with a Vincent spouse. I can't imagine what words he has. I mean, you just let us have our way, and all is well."

Erika laughed richly and hugged her grandmother again. "I missed you!"

"I hear laughter!" Liz sashayed into the room with Annie. They carried a wedding dress wrapped in plastic for safety, as well as the box of various accessories to go along with it. "I guess that means I won't get clawed this time. Bad kitty!"

Her friend winced wryly. "Sorry. At least you're better off than Luke. I think Gabriel bit his ankle while in a dog form."

"Which dog?"

"German Shepherd."

Annie winced. "Oops. I'll go make sure he's patched up, if another witch doesn't beat me there. Let's get you into this thing and make sure it all fits!"

For convenience, Erika put on her garter belt and stockings before they attempted to get her into the corset. It was unlaced entirely before being wrapped around her curvy body, and she held the front in place as Annie started lacing the ribbons back through the eyelets. The first tightening of the ribbons was no big deal. It was when Annie needed to actually pull them into proper position that things got interesting.

"Grab the footboard of the bed and try not to fall over. Or dislodge it," the elder witch instructed.

"It weighs a few hundred pounds," Liz retorted. "Can she move that?"

"She's half-vampyre, so, yes."

Erika grabbed the footboard and then held on for dear life as her mother yanked on the laces. "Who invented these ridiculous things?" she demanded. "Give me a bra any day!" Just because she was willing to wear one as a necessity did not strictly mean she found them to be practical. Almost exactly like pantyhose, really.

Annie ignored her. "Liz, grab the tape measure. We want her just tight enough to fit the dress but not make her uncomfortable."

Liz measured around Erika's waist and then said, "Another two inches."

"Sadists!"

"Shush, Erika." Annie made her way down

the ribbons to tighten them more. "Are you still able to breathe?"

"So far, yes. But I don't recommend going any further. I am not fainting at Gabriel's feet while giving our vows."

Liz quickly measured. "We're good." She stepped back to study Erika as Annie tied off the ends, and she sighed suddenly. "I should look so amazing in a corset. You are sexy as all get out, Erika. Gabriel might not survive your wedding night once he gets you out of your dress."

"He'll survive," Maria said serenely, "but he will be somewhat incoherent, at the least. And don't worry if he rips the ribbons. They've been torn twice now. I think it's a tradition, too."

Annie grinned a bit wickedly. "And it's rather sexy, I must say. Thomas is such a calm sort. Having him impatient enough to rip ribbons off my corset?" She sighed gustily. "I love getting him in that state."

"I feel so jealous now," Liz groused. "I need to find someone who wants me enough to rip a corset's ribbons."

"You'll find him or her eventually," Maria promised. "Now, let's get that dress onto Erika. It'll take all three of us."

A hoop skirt had to go on first, and then a

corset cover. Finally, the confection of cream and red satin and silk could be put on. It consisted of nearly fifty yards of total material, and it weighed more than it looked. The first layer was just the skirt that would barely skim the floor once Erika put on her low heels. The second layer was the rest of the dress that included the bodice and polonaise with its several foot long train.

The bodice fitted to the waist while just barely going past the edge of the corset on top, making it a bit more daring than was strictly traditional. The sleeves were tiered with sheers and laces and reached Erika's elbows. Little rosettes had been embroidered all down the edge of the polonaise and followed around back to the train.

"Can you breathe?" Maria asked Erika.

"Can you *walk*?" Liz amended.

Erika took a few steps and then smiled. "Yes and yes. It's not as bad as I thought. Do I look as amazing as I feel? I feel a bit like a princess, and I didn't know I wanted to feel that way." She let Annie bring her over to the full-length mirror, and she could only stare at her reflection. After a moment, she managed, "Forget the wedding night. Gabe might not survive the wedding *ceremony*. The train will be bustled up, right?"

"For dancing, yes." Annie wiped at her eyes. "Oh, damn it. I swore I wouldn't cry. You want Gabriel to see you now so he can get over the shock?"

"Yes, please. Tomorrow will be so busy that we won't have time for that 'first look' thing with us in our wedding clothes." She ducked a bit so that Maria could put the veil on her head. It was designed to flow back down over her hair rather than cover her face. Their kind had never really gone in for the modesty aspect, even centuries before. The term 'progressive vampyre' might sound oxymoronic but was humorously accurate in many ways.

The three women left her to fiddle with her curls a bit as they wanted to get caught in beading, and she turned with a smile when she heard the door open again. Gabriel stepped inside and then stopped dead in his tracks. She could only sigh contentedly as she studied her husband-to-be.

Much as he had protested the puffy shirt and snug breeches, there was no denying that he had the frame to pull them off *good*. He wore the same cream and red that she did, and had the same rosettes for embroidery. A heavy velvet jacket just emphasized his broad shoulders. She looked him over as thoroughly as he looked at her, and then she saw his feet and started laughing. He had on his beloved sneakers still. "I will pay you to wear those tomorrow!"

"Our parents would kill me. They have terrible toe pinchers set aside with your heels." He slowly reached out to catch her around the waist and flexed his fingers as if to hunt for the soft flesh beneath several layers of boning. "Do I dare ask what you have on under this?" he asked softly, his thickened voice belying his hunger.

"You'll find out after the reception." Her eyes softened as he changed his grip to hold her as if for a waltz. "I think maybe I'm becoming a fan of tradition. How about you?"

"It grows on you, certainly. But these pants never will."

She could only laugh. "At least I'll get you out of them soon enough." She leaned against his chest and listened to his heart beating. "What do you want for the future, Gabe? After our trip to Alaska, I mean."

"Well, I figure you will go back to academy to finish that degree of yours you want, and I'll start using mine to paint things that might have sale value." He let his fingers tangle in her hair. "After that, we can both dig in our heels and see if we can find our dreams. When you become famous and start traveling the world, the castle will be our home base, and I'll paint in the back of your tour bus while we're on the road." He added musingly, "I could handle being the trophy husband of a famous star."

"What if we never make it?" she teased.

"Then we accept our family fortunes and turn the castle into a tourist location. We can charge extra to be scared by ghosts." He stole a quick kiss. "I know we'll make it, Erika. Didn't that agent from the contest already contact you and say she wanted you in a studio after we're married?"

"Well, yes. But that's not a guarantee."

"Trust me," he urged. "I know you'll be there."

She looked up at him and then smiled. Words she might never have been able to say before came to her with utter ease. "I trust you." As his eyes glowed with happiness and he kissed her, she wondered again why those were the only words she could find. When would she be able to say she loved him?

Witches were up and running hours before sundown the following day to get a jumpstart on the wedding. Vampyres woke at the moment the sun set and grabbed breakfast on the run if they were involved with any part of the preparations. Others could wait for the reception. Erika got dragged out of her warm bed from her fiancé's side an hour before the sun set. Not easy for the half-vampyre, but she didn't need to be entirely awake for the first part of getting ready since it involved hair and makeup. The setting sun made her more alert, luckily.

The ceremony had been scheduled to begin at ten pm. Thanks to early sunsets that time of year, they had almost three hours to have everything in place. Annie took her time with Erika's curls and threaded thin strings of seed pearls through them. Liz handled makeup, ensuring to flatter everything about Erika's already beautiful face.

The castle doors stood open to invite any and every visitor to walk right in. Ushers stayed on hand to show people to the gardens where they could find seats. Many people made quick tours of the grounds before doing so; it was rare for Vincent Castle to open up in this manner, so villagers especially were curious.

Erika felt oddly happy and content over everything. She was just about to strip off her normal clothes to get into her wedding wear when the bedroom door opened and a very somber Lucas walked in. Her gut clenched with dread. "Luke?"

"I can't find Gabriel," he said bluntly. "Went to wake him in the tower when he didn't show up after sunset, and he wasn't there. No one has seen him. It's as if he just walked out of the castle and never came back. We're keeping it quiet, but . . . Erika, it looks one hell of a lot like you've just gotten stood up at the altar."

Slicing pain cut into Erika's chest for just a brief moment. It almost immediately got drowned in sheer, molten, fury. "The man is so set on marrying me," she bit out, "then that's what he's going to fucking do!" She shot to her feet. "He hasn't stood me up, Lucas. And if he has, I'm dragging him to that priest by the seat of his pants if needed!" Inside her mind, that mysterious door shook wildly as if something fought to get in. "Buy me an hour! We'll be back in time to get ready and get married, mark my words!"

"Erika!" Annie tried to protest, but it was too late. Erika had run out the door far faster than any witch could hope to catch. "Luke?" she whispered. "What's really going on? Where's Gabriel? What happened?"

"I only have a guess." He crossed his arms tightly and then uncrossed them to hug Liz when she moved closer. "The castle doors are wide open. Anyone could walk right inside. Say . . . even a cultist?"

"But Erika has been in here, safely, and there are several guards in the hall!" Maria protested. Her breath caught in understanding. "But there were no guards on Gabriel," she whispered. "And what better way to get Erika than to kidnap the man she loves? They just had to come in right before sunset after she had already left the tower. He was defenseless."

The same thought had already gone through Erika's mind. She had no desire to talk to anyone or be waylaid, so she turned into her favored cat form and navigated halls and people that way. She ran up to the tower bedroom she and Gabriel shared, and her sharp nose immediately caught a trace of something bad. She didn't even feel her fur bristle or hear her own hiss.

The door quivered again in her mind. This time, she willingly opened it. She came under immediate assault from a flood of emotions and thoughts that felt foreign. It took her a few seconds to realize they were *Gabriel's.* Everything he felt, everything he *was*, seemed to pour into her, and she saw directly into his heart. Where they had metaphysically left pieces of themselves inside each other before, the odd reciprocity of drinking each other's blood had *physically* left pieces of them inside each other. There was a piece of his mind inside her, and surely a piece of hers inside him.

She took a long breath. *Gabriel?*

There was no response, at least not in words. It was just a jumble of emotions and impressions. She could even briefly see what he did. It turned out to be enough. She could see thick trees in a circle around a grove. A dozen people in those familiar cloaks and masks of the cult. The full moon shining right down on the center of the circle. A stake with firewood heaped around it.

Hands suddenly grabbed his face. She could see out his eyes to see the masked face pressing in close. "I see her in your eyes," a mechanical voice said. "I know she sees me. Come to us, half-breed, or we stake him right here and now. You will burn, and we will live forever."

She pulled herself out of Gabriel's mind and felt all four of her legs trembling. She could feel him trying to shut the door between them but refused to let it happen. The location of the cult was not far. She could get there in only a few minutes if she flew.

A flying cat would entirely creep everyone out, so she instead stayed in the cat form until she reached just beyond the gardens where she could not be seen. She then returned to normal and lifted off the ground as she shot forward. This bullshit was long overdue to be finished!

No one had ever accused her of timidity or shyness. She landed when she found the clearing and then strode right into the middle of it. Her lips curled into a sneer as cultists leapt back in terror. "I'm here as you've wanted. The fact that you stole Gabriel *out of my bed* should be a clue that this is absolutely in waste! Let him go, you dumbasses, before I remind you why you've been after me!"

The one who seemed to be the leader moved closer to her and grabbed her wrist. "You will burn first!" He or she hauled Erika over to the stake and then lifted her onto the wood. "Don't do anything stupid!"

Erika kept her mouth shut as her arms were bound behind the stake. Her eyes met Gabriel's. Fear had made him paler than usual, and blood trickled down his lip from where someone had struck him. Only the wooden spike pressed against his chest kept him from struggling against the chains binding him. *It's okay,* she thought to him, and watched his eyes widen.

"Brothers and sisters!" the ringleader crowed. "Soon we will have what we deserve! This half-breed will burn, and we will take in her power! We will be immortal gods! No one will stand in our way!" They took the torch offered by another and dropped it onto the wood. "Burn! Burn and give us your power!"

She felt no fear whatsoever as the flames leapt, and her heart hardened with raw fury at the idea of how many others may have met their end that way. The worst way to go, really, and the most offensive one that could be used against anyone with witch blood. She watched the flames climb closer and closer to her feet . . . and then smirked when they seemed to stop in their tracks. "Uh-oh," she taunted, her musical voice beginning to resonate with power. "I see your magical flames know what you wouldn't accept. Really, you should have seen it the moment I arrived."

"Seen what?" the leader demanded.

"I'm wearing yellow."

The flames surged up toward her and then suddenly billowed backward like a wave pulling from shore. Screams rose as the flames surged outward in a shockwave. Some cultists were immediately engulfed and fell to writhe on the ground in burning agony. Others tried to run, but the flames followed them. One by one by one, every member of the cult was set on fire and left to immolate. Nothing else burned. Not the trees, not the leaves on the ground.

The leader tried to scramble away as the flames followed. A voice began to softly, almost sweetly, begin to sing, and all control over their body was lost. Even behind the mask, the leader's eyes filled with sheer horror as they turned toward the stake where Erika calmly stood. As sweet as her voice sounded, her eyes looked hard as gems. Flames grabbed the leader's feet and clothes and climbed their body. All that came out was one partially formed scream before the flames ate them alive.

Gabriel tore free of the chains holding him and ran across the ground past piles of ashes to reach the stake. He tore away the ropes binding Erika and then jerked her into his arms a bit desperately. All around them, the flames had started to die out. Nothing remained but ashes and bits of material. "Karmic backwash," he managed to say hoarsely.

"And now we know what happens when a sacrifice is not what he or she is supposed to be."

She threw her arms around his neck and held on just as tightly. "Are you okay? Did they hurt you?"

"Hit me once. I sassed the person in charge." He caught her face in his hands and searched her eyes. "I swear, Erika," he said unsteadily, "I would never, ever, have left the castle. I would never stand you up at the altar. It was all I could think when I woke up and realized what was going on. Tell me you believe me, that you never thought that!"

"Gabriel." She leaned up to kiss him tenderly. "I honestly never believed you would stand me up." Her lips curved. "And I think I told the others that, even if you had tried, I would not accept it. You would be marrying me if I had to drag you by your pants to the priest. Come on. We need to hurry. We still need to get ready! We have just enough time if we fly."

"Erika." He almost crushed her in his arms for a moment, too relieved to immediately let go. Something had changed inside her. He could see it, but he could not name it. There was just no time to dwell on it. It was barely an hour until the ceremony started!

It was to the credit of their family members that no one said a word when they showed up, and both were dirty and had ash on their shoes.

Annie healed up Gabriel's lip for him before he was absconded by the menfolk to get ready. The women then descended on Erika and worked at mach one to fix damage to her makeup and hair before stripping her and getting her into the many layers of her wedding clothes.

She stepped into her shoes and got her veil on five minutes before she and Gabriel were to meet at the end of the aisle to walk together. Liz hurried her through the castle to the exit into the garden, and Lucas came from the other direction hurrying Gabriel. Bride and groom met at the doors and then laughed.

"Glad someone is amused!" Liz complained. She smoothed out the skirts of her red gown and then adjusted the train on Erika's skirt. The familiar first chord played, and she gave Erika a quick kiss before accepting Lucas' arm so they could walk first down the aisle. At the end, they took their places beside the altar. The couple's wedding rings rested in their pockets, ready to be used.

The music continued, and the entire audience stood as Erika and Gabriel stepped out into the garden. She should have had a hand on his elbow, but their hands instead linked between them. Their free hands carried the red and cream ribbons that would be used to bind their wrists together.

They made it to the altar where the priest stood, and she cleared her throat with a smile. "Dear friends," she began, "we are gathered here tonight . . ."

And, so, they were married. The ribbons that bound their wrists were after tied to Erika's gown and Gabriel's jacket, later to be put in a box for safekeeping. When it came time to exchange rings and vows, Gabriel went first after they had put the rings on each other. He took a long breath and looked down into the blue eyes that had haunted him for three years and would now be with him for all time. "Erika. From the moment we met, I knew you were it. I made mistakes. I made a big one, and I thought I lost everything. Somehow we're here. You believed in me. You trusted me. And I vow here, for always, to always love you. To always be with you. To never betray you again. I will be there every sunrise to hold you as we sleep, and I will still be holding you when the setting sun wakes us again. I am yours for always ever after."

Erika looked up at him and felt her lips tremble. "I knew you were trouble. That moment I first saw you. Our first kiss was our first time making love. There's so much between us. And, yes, you hurt me. I thought I might never heal. But . . . we're here. The past is behind us, and the future is before us. I . . ." She trailed off and shook her head as the words simply refused to form. The vows she had carefully written just could not pierce the emotion welling. "I can't do this in this way. There's too much inside me."

"Then sing, songbird," he urged huskily. "It will come from your heart."

Her ringed hand tenderly cupped his cheek as she let the music well until it spilled from her beautiful voice in an unbreakable vow.

I will fly into your arms
If you will catch me
Fly away with me
To the ends of the world
Through winter
Through spring and summer
Until autumn comes again
Until our nights our endless
I am falling into you

She drew a long breath. "And," she added softer, "I will love you until the end of forever."

His breath caught and then he dragged her into his arms and kissed her with an unleashed fury of emotion. The audience burst into cheers and whistles. The very amused priest could only say, "Well, I'm supposed to tell them to kiss here as husband and wife, but I guess they beat me to it. Let's have a round of applause for the newly married couple!"

The reception that followed was held in the grand ballroom. Erika and Gabriel melted many hearts with their first dance, and they made themselves available to everyone who wanted to come up and give them warm wishes. The party continued on for two hours, and at midnight, Annie and Christina very competently began to show people out. Those who would still be spending the night made their way back to their rooms, and others left to either start journeying home, or to go back to the village.

It took another half an hour before Erika and Gabriel found themselves alone in the ballroom. The entire place looked a bit disastrous, yet it was a sign of a party highly enjoyed. The newlyweds sat at their table of honor and smiled at each other after a look around the place. "Did I see your cousin flirting with Liz?" Erika asked her husband politely.

"I really wanted to warn him that he's going to fall insanely in love with her, but that's not exactly a problem as far as I'm concerned. If she sounds hesitant, tell her he was a weight lifter at academy." He grinned when that made Erika laugh. "Another dance, my dear wife?"

"I'd love one." She let him tug her up and contentedly spun into his arms. "I'm not sure I can completely qualify this as the best day of my life, if only because the cult really did their best to botch that, and my life will be really long and should have other great days, but it's definitely at the top of my list so far."

He nuzzled her hair where curls escaped the veil. "I guess I ought to apologize for jumping the gun during the ceremony, but when you finally said you loved me still . . . well."

"I don't want an apology." She wound her arms around his neck and smiled. "Once I saw that door connecting us, saw that our minds were connected, my fears went away. I knew that I was flying, and if ever there was fear of falling, you would catch me. I trust you more than I ever did before, Gabe, if only because I truly, deeply, believe that you never meant to hurt me. Knowing that, I could say I loved you, as I've wanted to say for days."

"That door." He shook his head. "I can't believe you could do that."

Her lips curved. "Gabriel . . . I didn't make the

door. You did." She played with the hair at the nape of his neck as he stared at her. "We left pieces of ourselves inside each other, literally, when we shared blood the first time. You wanted so desperately, so terribly, to make me trust you, to show me that you would never hurt me . . . well, you basically made it so I could see into your mind at any time I wanted. Until I feared losing you, I didn't have the nerve to open the door. When I did . . . the first thing I wanted to tell you were those three most important words that are the strongest vow I could have ever made." Her lips touched his. "I love you. And I will love you forever."

He scooped her up into his arms and began to stride toward the doors. "I think it's time we started our honeymoon. We can leave for Alaska tomorrow night. Tonight is just us. I have no intentions of letting go of you, Erika."

She rested her head on his shoulder and smiled. "Until the dawn breaks?"

"Until time ends."

Her sigh sounded long and contented as she held him closer. There was no more danger, and any pain had been left in the past where it belonged. Their life would be periods of bliss pocketed with yelling, fighting, and magic spells, and she could truly think of nothing better. Everything had come out perfectly in the end. "That should be just long enough."

Fin

A*BOUT* T*HE* A*UTHOR*

Stacy J. Garrett was made in England but born in Sacramento, California, and like the redwoods of the state, her roots have dug deep. Her destiny as a bard was somewhat inevitable. Little else can explain how she constantly told her mother tall tales so outlandish that she couldn't even get grounded for them. Her mother and grandmother had her reading by age three, and that love of a good story propelled her through so many books that Scholastic Books gave her a medal. A love of worlds created by others eventually brought out the desire to create her own, and she has never looked back.

Stacy has seen both good and evil in her life, and her stories, like life, have no half measures. Even in a fantasy world of dragons and faeries, even in a modern city where magic abounds, she knows that the constants of real emotion never change. Dreams come true, love can be found at first sight, princesses can rescue their princes, and maybe there really can be happily ever after. Her happy endings never come without cost, though, for she truly believes we can't appreciate the good and the joy without the bad and the pain along the way.

Her current haunt is a comfy house in her beloved Sacramento where she wrangles three feline fur-kids and consumes peppermints like mana in order to balance a calendar filled with more creative venues than a sane person should realistically undertake. If she's not chained to her desk, she's stomping through the scenery in search of equally fantastical photographs.